BON VOYAGE, MRS FRAMPTON

BON VOYAGE, MRS FRAMPTON

Pam Gems

BLOOMSBURY

First published 1990
Copyright © 1990 by Pam Gems
The moral right of the author has been asserted

Bloomsbury Publishing Ltd, 2 Soho Square, London WIV 5DE

A CIP catalogue record for this book
is available from the British Library

ISBN 0 7475 0703 1

10 9 8 7 6 5 4 3 2 1

Typeset by Hewer Text Composition Services, Edinburgh
Printed in Great Britain by Butler and Tanner Ltd, Frome and London

Who ever would have thought it? Who could have imagined that after retiring to Spain and finding such a dear friend in May Liu, tragedy would strike, and Mrs Frampton would find herself on the move? Just when everything was going so well at Casa John Liu, the home for sick and handicapped children the two women had set up together, after Mrs Frampton's Vic died. They'd even had a visit from the Queen! Now everything had changed; Mrs Frampton wasn't even sure she was needed at Casa John Liu any more. She'd come a long way from Bradford (and she wasn't going back *there*) but where was home to be now?

It's the carpet of wild pansies in the front that makes her buy the run-down farmhouse in France, and the renovation gives her plenty to think about – for a while . . . If only she could bring herself to paint again. What is she waiting for? The unexpected arrival from Spain of May Liu's former chauffeur Honoré, in a state of distress, brings a new sense of purpose . . . no time to brood with a man to look after. But kindness, this time, has astonishingly rejuvenating rewards – and startling consequences, taking Mrs Frampton half-way round the world on an intriguing trail of self-discovery. Retired and alone she may be, but she's damned if she's going to stop living.

In this beguiling sequel to *Mrs Frampton*, Pam Gems's inimitable comic heroine keeps pages turning and hearts melting.

Chapter 1

MRS FRAMPTON LOOKED at her list, sucking at her front teeth. It was no use. She would have to go back into Marbella. There was the woman to see about the extra flower arrangements, the Greek lady with the cakes to chase up, and she would try once more to catch the headmistress to ensure the arrival of the school-children – no, no good hoping for the best – she would lay on a bus.

More expense but at least I know the little devils will be there on time.

Should they hold flowers . . . throw red carnations? She shook her head – perhaps better not to risk a poke in the eye.

And while I'm up at the school I can pop into Señora Santiago's for the new overalls and pick up the embroidered tablecloths, courtesy of the d'Oliviera sisters. It's all go!

Perhaps a coffee first. Coffee was on Dr Guttmann's forbidden list but half a spoon of Nescafé with skimmed milk, surely that wasn't going to whizz the blood pressure through the roof. Mrs Frampton stirred in the milk decisively and took her cup out on to the terrace to enjoy the balmy morning air.

Was there ever such air as this? Sweet and gentle on the face, with the faint fragrance of flowers. Undoubtedly there was more pollution with the increasing development along the coast. Why on earth didn't the government get on and build a decent autoroute up in the hills from Granada to Gibraltar? If they weren't careful they were going to kill the golden goose. People would move on. That was the way of it. Mammals used up a feeding ground and pushed off to new pastures.

We're no better than a herd of buffalo, thought Mrs Frampton, only now we're running out of territory, out of world, and I don't fancy pushing off to Mars.

1

She put her feet up on the basket chair and inspected her ankles. They were definitely down, not nearly so puffy since she had been back on the diet.

I expect they'll be up a bit tomorrow.

She sat back, smiling to herself. Who would have thought it? Who would have thought that I, May Frampton, would be meeting the Queen of Spain? Queen Sophia. Who was arriving, at eleven the next morning, to visit Casa John Liu, the residence for sick and handicapped children run in tandem by Madame Henri Liu and Mrs Victor Frampton.

Preparations had been in progress for a year. The Arab royals, in their *sotto voce* way, had donated a large slice of land for tennis courts and a track and the Marbella Club had paid for the swimming-pool extension. A new music room had been organised by the Mayor, with a splendid piano, curtains appliquéd with white doves, and a large sum raised by a series of winter festivities.

This last sum, coming as a splendid bonus, had created the necessity for heady decision. Both Mays had sat for hours in conference. The Spanish leaned towards the superb – even Mother Caterina and the Sisters were for making the residence a majestic and serene expression of the good, a noble example to act as a model. May Liu, a democratic chairwoman (with, Mrs Frampton suspected, despite her perfect manners, a low boredom threshold), seemed in the mood to give way to the grandiloquence invoked with prolonged Hispanic passion.

Mrs Frampton, who for almost an hour had not been able to get a word in, cleared her throat in the end and piped up. It wouldn't do, she said. They were all on the wrong tack. She couldn't, she wouldn't, she was not going to agree. Who were they all trying to impress – God?

At this gross impiety the room went quiet, so quiet that Mrs Frampton was able to press home her advantage. It was all very well to talk of walks and arches and tessellated courtyards. Yes of course the residents should not be deprived of beauty. But wasn't there already beauty enough? In flowers, in the trees, in the blue sky? Never mind plans for electronic wizardry in the dance room, talk of trips to Disneyland. There were, she said, looking round the table at everyone in turn, more important battles to be fought.

After losing her voice in the long debate that followed, she won the vote overwhelmingly. A vote to use the money to bring in short-stay patients, children who needed rest and recuperation with their parents after serious operations, cancer therapy, treatment for burns. Let us share more widely, she had said. And Mother Caterina had compressed her lips with a short nod, given Mrs Frampton a dark look and lifted an authoritative finger. The Sisters followed suit and afterwards surrounded Mrs Frampton for a shy moment before dispersing with their usual spectral silence.

Now the Queen was coming. The newspapers had been full of it.

We're going to have to be careful, thought May to herself. If we get too fashionable we'll be dead duck next year.

She voiced her worries to Little May, who smiled and teased her.

'You don't want to be a media star?'

'I'll leave that to Antonio.'

Antonio, of the misshapen face and body, one of the residents, had been given a small role in a film the previous year. A second unit, shooting exteriors and action sequences in the hills behind Estepoña, had needed unusual faces for a confrontation between a haughty bishop and a country priest and his peasant flock. Something honest and real about Antonio's demeanour in his few scenes in ruff and doublet – his grotesque appearance having fired the director into giving him a small role – had caught the national imagination when the film, a serious and poignant story, had been a box-office success. Antonio's own story, his abandonment in a haycart in infancy, his discovery by children who had fed the hideous baby for several days before taking him to the local priest, became food for newspapers and magazines and the camera. Antonio, with Sister Lourdes acting as interpreter since his speech was esoteric, gave many interviews. The payments for these were being used to rebuild his jaw and give him a decent dentition. This he was enduring with laconic stoicism.

3

Antonio, the nuns had long discovered, was not only of normal but of high intelligence. His work in the grounds of the residence was creative and ambitious, involving much earth-moving. Now, aided by young Bedir, the Arab gardener, he was making a complicated water garden of pumps and fountains. Mrs Frampton, dwelling on the new stepped parterres which would – just – be ready in time, sighed pleasurably. Then she rose, making the basket chair squeak, her sigh modulating to a groan. It was all very well to dwell on past achievement. She let out an even louder groan and went to find her sunhat.

When her friend May Liu, widow of a Hong Kong tycoon, had given her beautiful house to be a home for convalescent children and the handicapped, Mrs Frampton, taking on the job of senior matron, had thought of giving up her own small, comely house in the Pueblo La Jolla. At first she had been too busy to make the necessary arrangements for a sale – there was no time to do more than dash home from time to time for a rest, for an hour of peace and quiet. Those occasionally snatched hours, half-mornings, ends of afternoons, had decided her not to sell. She needed her house. Taking on a senior post at her age was one thing. Keeping going was another. You had to pace yourself. It was no good rushing. Whatever the crisis, she could not tear about as she had when, to help her husband establish his business, she had carried on as a theatre sister as well as rearing two children and running a household. The legs weren't there any more – though the blood pressure was! She tried to acquire the Spanish indolence when, at the beginning, so much went wrong . . . permissions delayed, rooms flooding, builders defaulting . . . but derelictions meant more breaches to be filled, more contretemps to be resolved.

Now, with Casa John running smoothly at last, and with Little May in silent and imperturbable command, it was time to show off; to display the achievements of residents and staff, to inform the public of what was possible in the care of the needy. The visit of the Queen would be the jewel in the crown. Royal approval would have a wide and influential effect. Mrs Frampton gave her Crimson Glory rose, flowering itself into the vine, a last fond look. Yes, there were masses of buds. She would make a special bouquet for Fernanda, the young polio patient, to give to the Queen. If that didn't get Fernanda up on her feet nothing would.

The morning of the Queen's visit dawned gloriously. Mrs Frampton, up early in her small bright room at Casa John, showered and dressed quickly and made her morning rounds. By ten o'clock, panic was threatening to damage morale. The first to succumb were the infant out-patients, who all began to wail and howl and damage their parents' best clothes. Then the older children picked up the infection and became mischievous and restless and tiresome. Only Little May, in her cream silk suit, smiled gently and calmed not only the children but the younger nuns, source of the malaise, who were becoming tearful with nerves. Not so the day nurses from the agency who, prinking and giggling in the dispensary, tweaked their caps and applied discreet eyeshadow and lipstick. Mrs Frampton, delayed by several small crises, regained her room at last to throw on her new navy suit, her seed pearls (present from her son, Michael) and the new Baku straw hat.

And suddenly everything happened! And so quickly that time seemed to break into a run, leaving not a moment to dwell, to savour, to contemplate, before the swift scenario, so endlessly and lovingly prepared, was over.

The royal party arrived, purring to a halt at the main steps exactly on time. A comely woman in red with a small white cloche stepped out of the car and shook hands, and waited, smiling, as young Fernanda lurched slowly forward. The last few steps became a stumble and the Queen stepped forward instinctively and caught the child up in her arms, creating a photograph which flashed around the world and made a fortune for polio support groups everywhere. The tour proceeded without a hitch. Antonio was introduced, and displayed the gardens; the sick children were visited and the gymnasium and swimming pools inspected. The Queen drew aside for a short consultation and accepted a glass of the local Lanjaron water. She listened, she made notes, she exchanged information. More wards were visited, and the children from the local schools (rounded up punctually, thanks to Mrs Frampton's deliberate misinformation to the bus drivers as to the time of the royal arrival) sang cheerfully. All too soon, the quiet figure climbed back into the dark-blue car and was gone. The schoolchildren, noisy with joy at being given a holiday for the rest of the day, departed in their buses, waving and singing, and, as the patients settled down to lunch, Mrs Frampton lured Little May into the private sitting-room for a quiet tray.

'We deserve it.'

Little May smiled and put her feet up and allowed one of the girls to bring food from the kitchens.

'It's not that I'm a royalist,' said Mrs Frampton, her mouth full. 'I mean, you can't believe in it . . .'

'Because it is illogical?'

'Exactly. I mean, only the first-born, *if* it's a boy – '

'With the Arabs the most suitable is chosen.'

'Oh yes.' Mrs Frampton's tone was tart. 'With all those poor women in the background breeding away. My word, think of the pushing and shoving . . . for power, I mean, not literally.'

Little May giggled, putting her hand over her mouth. She always enjoyed Mrs Frampton's jokes.

'No,' said Mrs Frampton, leaning forward to take a bread roll and deciding against it. 'You can't take royalty seriously. Still. When you see people rise to the occasion – '

'I agree. To see a task performed perfectly . . .'

'Exactly.'

They ate for a while without speaking. Mrs Frampton looked across at her friend, her dear friend picking lightly at her chicken salad. How much they had been through together! Here was Little May, in her fifties, her wealth given over to the Casa John Liu and the farm in the hills, and I couldn't even bring myself to sell my house! Still, I paid for the physiotherapy department and the other bits and pieces – the gardening bills were heavy enough, thanks to Antonio's typically Spanish grandee notions. Giving was the virtue. Was it wrong to do it in a way which pleased yourself, gave you some fun? Yes, probably, if less was achieved for those in need. Mrs Frampton, her energies reviving with the egg custard, decided none the less to forgive herself. It

6

had been a wonderful morning. Fernanda's stumble with the flowers had turned everyone's heart, there had been no collisions in the ambitious dancing display, the new fountains had surged splendidly into life just at the moment that the Queen stepped forward to open the new gymnasium extension.

'What of this afternoon?' murmured Little May. 'What *can* we do?'

'I know.'

They sighed in unison.

'You were clever to arrange outings.'

'I thought of it when I was ordering the buses for the school. It seemed sensible, with everyone all dressed up, and it will give some of the staff a rest.'

'What shall *we* do?'

'Oh, nothing less than a state ball. The Nobel prize, perhaps?'

'What about a sauna?'

Mrs Frampton was not keen on the sauna, which tended to make her feel ill. She shook her head.

'Do you know, I think I'll just go home and put my feet up, read a magazine. If I were you, I'd do the same, lie low for a bit.'

'Perhaps. Maybe a sauna and massage later.'

'Good idea,' said Mrs Frampton drowsily. She rose, feeling sleep about to overtake her, picking up her bag and the trays. Little May looked up, smiling.

'Be careful.'

'I'm all right.'

Mrs Frampton looked down at the delicate face.

'Take it easy, May.'

Little May nodded.

'Yes, May. And you.'

Mrs Frampton was deeply asleep on her bed, dreaming that she was putting out little gold ballroom chairs round the pool at Dr Guttmann's slimming clinic. There was a sudden black, ominous something, then screaming, and then the glass doors between the exercise room and the pool stood up and tilted towards her and shattered, spiking light around her head. She sat up with a choking gasp. The screaming of her dream was the telephone, shrill by her bed.

'Yes?'

'Señora Frampton . . . oh, Señora Frampton!'

'What is it, what's the matter?'

'Oh, Señora Frampton – '

But the Sister seemed to be crying. There was a clattering sound, and then another voice came on the line. It was Mother Caterina, her deep tone even more abrupt than usual.

'Señora, please come at once.'

'What is it?'

'There has been an accident.'

Chapter 2

DRIVING QUICKLY ALONG the Carretera de Cádiz, Mrs Frampton overtook a lorry which hooted loudly. She glanced at the speedometer, took her foot off the accelerator. She was getting as bad as the other drivers on this wretched dangerous road who all, as soon as she lessened speed and settled into the slow lane, surged past her. An accident. Sister Concepción had sounded hysterical, but then she was always a nervous woman. More ominous had been the tone in Mother Caterina's voice. There was no hysteria there. And on such a day. What a shame. She slowed down and turned up the winding road to the residence, past the groves of eucalyptus and the heavy swathes of long-leaved mimosa trees. The gates of the residence were open as usual, the days when you had to be vetted by the lodge-keeper were well past. Now the world was welcome at Little May's house. It was no longer the retreat of a reclusive, shy woman, imprisoned by her own wealth. That wealth was fertilising a dozen useful projects, far beyond Málaga Province. Mrs Frampton slowed down and took the curve through the gates with expertise.

Something happened. Something dreadful. The feeling was so strong, so black, so awful, that Mrs Frampton's control of the car was lost completely. There was a screaming in her head, unbearably high and prolonged. It was the dream she was having when the telephone had rung. There was a roaring, and then blackness. Slowly, very slowly, the screaming receded. Mrs Frampton struggled up, lifting her head which was resting against the side window. She found she had come to a halt on the broad verge. Across the grass on a far terrace sat Antonio, motionless, his neck out like a gargoyle. Further off stood Little May's favourite basket chair, with something bright, probably a

9

towel, draped across its back. Whatever was the matter? What had happened?

Take your time, May, take your time. Now, what is it?

Her arms seemed too heavy to move.

Have I had a coronary? A stroke?

She took a deep breath, timidly at first, afraid of the roaring, the screaming. The heaviness seemed to die away. She lay back, eyes closed. Only the faint smell of tea roses invaded. A bird twittered a harsh alarm close by in the hibiscus. Mrs Frampton turned her head carefully. There was no pain, no tightness in her chest. She moved her body, bending forward over the seat belt. Nothing wrong. The car had stalled. She turned the key and backed slowly off the grass and on to the drive.

Never mind. See to this later.

She drove shakily up the winding road in second gear. As the front of the house came into view, Mother Caterina appeared on the wide, shallow steps, Sister Rocio at her elbow. The Sister's face, never highly coloured, was like a white balloon. Mother Caterina looked strange, unlike herself, with an expression that Mrs Frampton had never seen before. She knew this woman's fierce nature, the inner battles, the scepticism, even the sardonic humour that was not always successfully masked. But she had never seen her like this before, with a mien so repellently black as to be almost devilish.

She looks as though she's just had a postcard from hell.

What could it be? They had nursed enough sad cases, heads together over the bed of a dying infant, or a clear-eyed child facing the knowledge of lonely death. Before she reached the bottom step she called out to the waiting women.

'What is it?'

Caterina, above her, looked down with a sudden gaze of such love, of such pity, that Mrs Frampton burst into tears.

'What . . . what?'

Sister Rocio swooped forward, collapsing into Mrs Frampton's arms.

'Our provider has been taken from us!'

Mrs Frampton stepped back, so that the Sister slipped and almost fell. As she teetered, throwing out a hand to right herself,

Mrs Frampton looked up at Mother Caterina. Who looked at her, with the strange expression, rigid, almost sneering with the effort to speak.

'Madame Liu is dead.'

The roaring came back into her head, and the screaming. Mrs Frampton fell back on to the gravel, before they could reach her, in a faint. The two women carried her into the house, and staunched the graze on her cheek. Struggling awake, she tried to push them away. She sat up, and the Sister pushed her down, forcing her head between her knees. There she stayed as they tended her face and the cut on her hand, their voices hissing softly behind her as they padded to and fro.

She heard herself say in a loud voice, 'How?'

Mother Caterina, crouching on her knees, came round to face her.

'A car accident.'

'Car accident,' echoed Mrs Frampton helplessly. 'A car accident?'

'Another car, at speed, turning left.' She seemed almost unable to speak, to breathe. She cleared her throat and went on, very low. 'She knew nothing. The other car hit sideways . . .' Her voice trailed away.

'What about Duvalier . . . Honoré?'

Caterina shook her head.

'He is in the clinic. I don't know. The car caught fire.'

'Find out,' said Mrs Frampton in a hostile voice. She looked up with a glare. 'Isn't somebody finding out?'

Sister Rocio said timidly, 'Sister Isabella and Sister Remedios are with him.'

Mrs Frampton struggled to her feet.

'Where is she? I want to see her.'

The nuns were still, as if suddenly turned into black sculptures in the pale ante-room. Caterina rose heavily, favouring her knees.

'Not now. Now you must come with me.'

The authority in her voice was both subduing and comforting, and Mrs Frampton followed her to the dispensary where Pilar, the young doctor on duty, inspected the cheek wound and

11

advised rest. She took the medication prescribed and, together with Mother Caterina, went to her little bedroom at the end of the first-floor corridor. The nun bent before her and took off her shoes, and helped her remove her jacket. She threw back the light counterpane.

'I don't want to go to bed.'

But the nun lifted up her legs and tucked the sheet around her. May immediately sat up.

'I don't want to lie down.'

'Please. There is nothing you can do. I shall stay with you.'

She sat apart on a chair, her hands in her lap. There was silence.

Mrs Frampton said, 'I want to see her.'

'Not now.'

'I have to see her!' She sat up and began to flail her arms frantically . . . The nun rose and stood over her.

'You cannot see her. The car caught fire. She is gone.'

On the dread word fire, her voice changed and she turned her face away. Suddenly, together, both women began to wail and howl, out of control. May rose and crossed the room and clutched Caterina, gasping with loud, roaring groans. Sister Rocio, terrified, rushed into the room. She stood, helpless, her hands waving, then closed the door and stood against it to repel intruders, the tears running down so copiously that her face shone in the sunlight.

Mother Caterina began to mutter prayers in a cracked, mannish voice, and May's low, weird howling gave way to a sobbing which went on and on and on. It seemed as though it would never end, as though there were no way of stopping it, ever. At the door, Sister Rocio, over and over, murmured consolation.

'It is right . . . it is right in the eyes of God to grieve . . . God will permit us to grieve for our sister . . . it is right . . .'

At long, long last the room was silent. Mother Caterina whispered to Rocio who went out and returned with further medication and a glass of milk. May took the sedative obediently and lay down on the counterpane, turning her face to the wall.

The dream was the same. She was putting out the golden chairs, row upon row around the swimming pool, in bright

12

sunshine. She woke, panting, as the blackness roared in again and the high screams wrenched her awake.

'She couldn't get out! She can't get out . . . she keeps turning the handle and she can't get out!'

Then the sedatives invaded once more and she dozed and woke, dozed and woke again, forcing herself awake this time and sitting up with a sudden determination. The sedatives were blocking off all feeling. She felt clear-headed, competent and matter-of-fact.

There's everything to do.

First, May's daughter Cinthia would have to be informed. Then lawyers, trustees, the Town Hall and the Mayor and the *presidente* of the local pueblo. Mrs Frampton put on her shoes and went down to the main office, brushing aside the nun at her door, to find the Mayor and the Chief of Police, their faces deep in misery. At the sight of her the young Mayor turned away his face to hide his tears. She put a hand on his arm.

'We've lost our dear one,' she said. And sat down.

It wasn't true, of course. It was a dream, a horrible dream. How could it be true? Of course it wasn't true.

What was amazing was the way you could keep going. She was even able to eat. Nothing tasted of anything but she stoked up at mealtimes, or forgot and noticed nothing. She felt neither tired or hungry. There was just this remorseless feeling of jobs needing to be done, of routines to be maintained, formalities to be enacted and disposed of, endless lists to be crossed out and discarded. Cinthia, arriving from Washington, was met at Málaga airport and escorted to the clinic to visit Honoré. Who lay, silent and still, looped about with machinery. One arm was undamaged and they sat, each in turn holding his hand lightly. Mrs Frampton spoke to him in her accented Spanish, telling him that he was recovering, that he must fight, that they needed him. She lied, saying that Madame Liu was doing well. Cinthia, who was holding his hand at the time, said afterwards that there had been a slight response at the mention of her mother's name. But Mrs Frampton sighed, doubting it, and she and Cinthia went away.

John's sons arrived with their mother, together with Cinthia's

13

husband and son and daughter, for the funeral. When it was announced that this would be private there was such a local, even national, outcry that Cinthia bowed to pressure. A public ceremony was arranged and the world came to honour the woman from Hong Kong who after the death of her son had given her billions to the care of the needy. Who had become, in three short years, a legend in Spain, and a model for others to copy.

At first Mrs Frampton had asked to be allowed to stay at home on the day of the funeral. She had begun to have strange feelings and was worried about her capacity to behave normally. But Cinthia, with Little May's soft, perceptive eyes, had lowered her lids and sighed gently, just like her mother. And Mrs Frampton, sensing her pain, had said, 'Of course I'll be there. We'll be together. I don't know what I was thinking about.'

So they followed the little hearse (what was in it . . .? There was nothing left, the police had said) to the church and to the graveside. Cinthia and Mrs Frampton shook hands with royalty, with ministers and representatives, with everyone who had come to pay respects and whisper consolation. It seemed as if the day would never end. When it did, Mrs Frampton drove Cinthia in the Volvo to the clinic, and they sat with Honoré. Who still did not know that his employer and friend was dead.

After, in the car, Cinthia spoke of her mother's will. Mrs Frampton had helped to draft it, remaking her own will at the same time. Cinthia stressed her support for her mother's wishes, and her determination that they should be fulfilled. She would, in time, take away the family treasures that her mother had bequeathed and the mementoes for the children and friends. She would act as trustee in her mother's place; the family connection would be maintained. Her husband's political career kept her in Washington, but who knew, perhaps one day one of John's sons or one of her own children might like to be part of the John Liu Foundation. Mrs Frampton listened to the soft voice and nodded, but could say nothing.

Cinthia stayed for several weeks, and then flew home, a bad day for Mrs Frampton, who, finding in the daughter something of

14

the mother, not least in the cadences of her voice, had begun to cling, even following her from room to room for no reason. It was hard, too, to say goodbye to the children. They clung, and she clung. They looked puzzled and their smiles were worried.

In the car going home from the airport, she wept softly. And Luis García, the sturdy widower, her neighbour in the pueblo who had asked her to marry him, murmured consolation.

Chapter 3

Mrs Frampton put down the telephone, pulling a face. Another disappointment. Chloe was not coming. With a third and unexpected pregnancy soon after the birth of her son Tom she had been advised not to travel.

'Not for another month, preferably two, the doctor says.'

'He's right. Why so soon? You haven't gone Catholic, have you?'

'No, just absent-mindedness. I get in a muddle with Patrick being away on assignments so often. Listen, why don't you come to us? It would do you good.'

'I can't.'

'Why not?'

'Honoré.'

'How is he?'

'Not good.'

Mrs Frampton went through to the sitting-room and sat by the window with her sewing. This was now her favourite place. From the window she could look out to sea across her small front garden, dressed simply with grass not to obscure the view. Beyond was the wide public garden framed by stone pines, and the smaller pueblo pool with its white tables and chairs. There was always someone sitting there . . . anyway, you never felt alone in the pueblo. Lucca and José, the young barmen, padded to and fro, Emilio, the porter, went about his business, and Maria-Claudi and Silvana, the maids, chattered and shrieked and sang as they carried their bright plastic buckets from dwelling to dwelling. She could sit outside herself, all day if she chose, with the other residents. But the light was trying, and in any case, she preferred to be alone.

I've done it again! Used the wrong colour!

16

She dug at the stitches with her needle, unpicking the wool. This was her new obsession, gros point, the latest a cushion cover of a hen with yellow chicks on a deep-blue background. It was a present for her daughter-in-law, the Australian Steffi, who had shown a surprising love of the traditional since the birth of her son, Sam. Mrs Frampton sent off lace and old damask pieces, made careful packages of anything old for the house in New England.

Michael had flown to be with her in the first months, his time, now that he was back on pure research, more his own, though he rang Boston daily to enquire after his lab cultures. They had talked endlessly through the nights when sleep abandoned Mrs Frampton altogether. The first serene, numbed shock had disappeared all too quickly, to be followed by feelings of such multiplicity that Mrs Frampton feared to leave the house, sensing a loss of control, a risk that she might . . . what? Start to scream aloud . . . be unable to move, start to laugh or cry in public – even worse, the most ominous fear of all, that she might be impelled to attack someone. Suppose she found herself setting about a child in the street . . . going for a blameless old woman, kicking out at a policeman? The thoughts came like grinning cats in the night or unexpectedly when she was polishing or making her bed.

Finding herself unable to work she had invoked friends and neighbours, begging them to take on voluntary commitments and responsibilities. Even the three Frenchwomen, her special bane from the other end of the pueblo, agreed to take on routine visits, though not for long. It wasn't their way. Beanpole, the pack leader, was bossy and critical and made the children cry, Pink (the erstwhile Henna) Rinse, her whining ally, emptied rooms of the chronically sick with sagas of split ends and broken fingernails, and Daftie, number three, could not open a tin without destroying the surgical ward, and once fed the blood bank to the cat.

For a boon of three weeks Michael took over. He drove Mrs Frampton to the clinic, and, sharing her fears for his progress, arranged for Honoré's removal to Madrid. Mrs Frampton stayed in the capital until she felt calmer about Honoré's condition. Now she was back in San Pedro and Michael had gone home.

17

Honoré, she was assured and reassured, was making a recovery. She stabbed violently at the canvas, compressing her mouth. What they told her was all very well. Nothing but words. Where was the rotund, seal-like and imperturbable Frenchman whose crisp interjections had so often been a call to common sense, who had been an integral part of the Casa John Liu? In the hospital he lay mutilated, concave and silent. His sisters had been to visit him and left, handkerchiefs to their eyes. He was the youngest, the one beloved boy. They wrote and sent him food that he could not eat, books that he could not read. Mrs Frampton made the journey to Madrid once a fortnight.

'Patience . . . patience, Señora,' said the doctors. Progress, could she not see, was steady.

Small, you mean, she thought.

The fact was, Honoré was not recovering.

He's lost his spirit. He doesn't *want* to live!

Mrs Frampton knew that he blamed himself for the accident. Despite all the evidence, despite the reassurances of authorities and friends, the crippled, blank-eyed Frenchman remained mute and inconsolable. Only once had he spoken directly to Mrs Frampton of the accident. He was, he said, in charge of the car. In charge of the protection of Madame Liu. It had been his sacred trust, his love, and the meaning of his life. He had failed in that trust. To which Mrs Frampton had made no answer. She shared in his misery – in his guilt, in his remorse. If only, if only she had agreed when May had suggested a visit to the sauna on that dreadful day – laziness and selfishness had stopped her. May had wanted to go – May, who so rarely expressed a direct wish. Why hadn't she gone instead of putting herself, her own comfort, first? If she had said yes they would have been on the road at a different moment, at a different spot. The accident would not have happened.

Despite Michael's patient reasoning the thoughts persisted. She felt as unable to come to terms with the accident as Honoré. She felt sullen, unwilling to speak to friends and neighbours. It was as if everything had changed, her capacity to eat, sleep, read, do her work, travel, shop, look after her house and affairs. And there were uglier thoughts. Thoughts of relief, even triumph that she had not been in the car herself, had not been burned to death, was alive, unlike the woman she loved, apart from her family, more than anyone else in the world, her best, her dearest friend.

These thoughts added to the strangeness within. During the first few weeks there had been odd and persistent feelings of Little May's presence. Not only of her presence but of her terrifying and unforgiving anger. Little May was in a deadly rage. She came to Mrs Frampton in the night, her face set as it had been during the months when, though the courts dismissed the charges for lack of evidence, she knew her son to be guilty of drugs trafficking. That face loomed, yellow and set, with black, blazing eyes. Mrs Frampton began to be frightened. She began to stammer, and not hear what was said to her. But then Little May went away. And that was worse. Mrs Frampton's feeling began to cohere into a deep rage of her own. She was abandoned. Her friend had left her. What about all the work to be done? How would she manage?

I can't do it on my own!

The glowing resentment fastened in deeply, like a tick on her neck. She began to go for long walks with Pompey, the pueblo dog, who had turned up one morning and, after being shooed off by Emilio, had caught two large rats and been given pride of place in the café. Her energy began to come back. But it wasn't right. It was as if the energy had been dislodged, was now in the wrong place. Nothing was certain any more. Nothing could be trusted. She found herself arguing over change in shops, complaining about noise, traffic, the number of people in the beach cafés, the over-development behind the town. Even her garden, usually an inducement of calm and reflection, failed to give consolation. The weeds seemed to grow faster than ever. Clouds of white fly flew up from the strawberries, the orange tree was covered in scale insect, small snails decimated the dahlias and even the long strands of the Crimson Glory rose were powdered with mildew.

'Come home,' said Chloe on the telephone. 'You're not yourself, Mum.'

'I'm all right.'

'No, you're not all right.'

But Mrs Frampton, willing to suggest professional help for others, dismissed it for herself. She knew that she was wrong. That her head was wrong. That everything had gone on the slew, gone sideways inside. She cut down her work at the residence, not because of lack of energy, but because she was not sound. She was unreliable. Fortunately, Mother Caterina seemed to understand. She would nod briefly and make rearrangement without discussion.

One small incident, on a hot day, made Mrs Frampton decide, suddenly and irrevocably, that the time had come for her to leave Spain. It happened on the day of Gudrun's wedding to Luis García. Gudrun, who had lived with a Swedish painter and nursed him through long years of illness, had slowly drawn close to Luis. After Mrs Frampton had turned down the lonely widower's offer of marriage in order to devote herself to the Casa John Liu, he had turned to Gudrun. Who had smiled, and jumped into bed with him cheerfully. Their affair became the talk of the pueblo until somehow Gudrun's frankness and direct common sense defused the gossip. From an item Gudrun and Luis became a fixture, now ratified, with Gudrun obligingly taking instruction and converting to Catholicism.

'Well, what is the difference?' she said with her slow smile, making Father Ignacio look in his lap.

But the hurdles were overcome, the guests invited, the cake baked, the flowers ordered and the dresses made. The pueblo looked forward to a celebration after the recent sadness, and Mrs Frampton determined that, on the surface at least, she must show a pleasant face. She went to her favourite antique shop and bought the pieces of blue-and-white china that Gudrun had coveted for over a year, and a silver-topped cane for Luis.

Chapter 4

THE DAY OF the wedding was tryingly hot. It was August, the only time of year not to be in Marbella if you were a resident. This was when the locals went north, renting out their homes to cover yearly maintenance costs, and leaving the beaches and pools to the swarm of northern Europeans restricted to children's holiday schedules. Because of the wedding Mrs Frampton had delayed her plans to go to England and her daughter. Now the thought of green Somerset became urgent and gave her the energy to pack.

The ceremony, in the coolness of the local church, was simple and pleasant. By the end of the celebrations, however, after standing in the sun for the protracted farewells, Mrs Frampton was in every way exhausted. She felt a dreadful lowness begin to invade, induced partly by envy of Gudrun's happiness, which might have been her own (but I had Little May then!) . . . and partly by waves of physical nausea. This she was now suffering frequently. The bright, harsh sun of the south seemed to threaten. The colours of the flowers which she had earlier found so glowing and vibrant now struck her as coarse and lacking in subtlety. The sun saw too much. The sagging faces of ageing men and women with their heavy buttocks, globular veins, thinning scalps and burnt noses upset her and made her sneer. You got ugly when you got old. Some did better than others. It depended on the luck of the draw, and how your health held out. There were those who flew to old age and those who fought it like lions, butchering and cropping their faces to the skull.

We can't win, though, can we? What are we all doing here? We look ridiculous. The south belonged to the Spanish, not the Dutch, the Germans, the English.

She would sit in the cafés watching the locals, the men wiry and dark-eyed, the women with their superb carriage, listening to the guttural sounds that she had tried so hard to copy without success.

It's me that's wrong. I'm the one out of place.

Was she . . . truthfully . . . needed? The residence, so dreadfully shaken by the loss of Little May, was rallying. Mother Caterina had discovered a new administrator, a short, stocky Polish woman who was proving invaluable and who had moved in and settled without waves.

'I like here.'

She had married an Italian, been unable to leave Poland until her husband, after eleven years of separation, was diagnosed with a fatal complaint. Now alone, her passion for her new post was touching.

I shan't be missed, thought Mrs Frampton.

She spoke to Mother Caterina. Who looked at her keenly and said, 'You must make voyage.'

'Yes,' said Mrs Frampton, 'but what . . . where?'

The Mother Superior had merely shrugged dismissively.

It's all very well for you, thought Mrs Frampton, you've got your religion.

Her own beliefs came and went, changing in depth and intensity. Just now it seemed that there was nothing, a void in every dimension. Perhaps the Hindus were right and Little May had become a drop in a limitless ocean. On the other hand, if reincarnation were true, perhaps she was already a baby in someone else's arms. Perhaps . . . but in any case, none of it carried consolation. That set of values, those quirks of character, that countenance, that whole which had been May Liu, was gone, erased, no longer existed. Leaving a venomous void.

After the smiling couple left the pueblo, Mrs Frampton veered away from the laden tables and joking groups of guests and, whistling for Pompey, slipped indoors to change her Baku straw for an old sunhat. Feeling herself to be bad company, she decided to go for a walk. It was no good. She wasn't in

22

the mood. The party would now get noisy, there would be music and dancing, plaintive songs into the night, jokes told, improprieties committed. What had it got to do with her? How could they sit there laughing, telling dirty stories? Gudrun had been mistaken to wear pink. Her hips had looked enormous, silly woman. Better to walk it off, all the shallow silliness, people enjoying themselves.

She crossed the main road, that devilish killer of a road, after waiting for the traffic to thin, and took off up one of the small tracks between vineyards and olive groves.

I dare say *they* won't be here much longer. They'll all be theme parks, or condominiums. Or another great supermarket.

She plodded up the dusty path, head down with her eyes on the burnt brown grass, the shucked seedheads and hard, dry earth. After walking for fifteen minutes she began to feel more at peace. The dog ran ahead, sniffing into the gateways of farms, bounding after birds and looping round her feet happily.

'Get out of it, Pompey . . . you'll have me over!'

But he was a sensible dog and never tried you too far. He took off down a track bordered by locust trees and Mrs Frampton followed. There was a farm and a ford at the bottom, dry at this time of the year. She would go that way, and across by the reservoir and back.

As she approached the farm, she heard the unearthly braying of a donkey, and then a man's voice shouting. Diverting from the path, she walked round the side of the farmhouse where a small, heavily built man was attempting to persuade his donkey to climb the steep rise from the field below. The donkey was pulling a cart full of bricks. As it heaved and slipped back and heaved again, the man lashed at its shoulders unmercifully. The donkey lifted its head and made its awful sound and was beaten again, and slipped back, and heaved, and surged forward. And slid back. As it did so it turned its head slightly towards Mrs Frampton, rolling its eyes in what seemed to be a look of human desperation . . . a kind of puzzlement that, though it was doing its best, punishment was its only reward. Mrs Frampton lurched forward and snatched the whip from the astonished farmer.

'You devil, stop that! I'll do it to you!'

23

She struck out at the man, catching him on the side of the face, causing him to stumble, more in surprise than from the weight of the glancing blow.

The donkey slid back to the bottom of the rise. And stopped. Its flanks were wet and shone in the sun like the quarters of a racehorse. Mrs Frampton, feeling the heat beating down on her forehead, dropped the whip. She went to the cart and began heaving off bricks, the man murmuring protest behind her. Then he too began to take off bricks, stacking them on the ground by hers until, panting, Mrs Frampton said in Spanish, 'And now, Señor, if you please, with God's help, try once more.'

But there were still too many. The donkey moved forward. And slid back down the shining hard-baked earth. They took off more bricks, working side by side. This time the donkey made it to the yard of the farm, through the mangled old gates. A boy emerged from an outhouse and started to unload without speaking, his dark eyes on Mrs Frampton in wonder. Mrs Frampton, her strength now evaporating, began to feel ill. The farmer jerked his head towards the farm door and she went inside, into cool darkness, and accepted a cup of water.

'You should not beat the animal.'

'The animal is for work.'

'It is foolish to give the animal work that it cannot perform.'

'Señora, I have work that I cannot perform. I have five children to feed.'

'It is still wicked to beat a dumb animal.'

'The Señora is inglesa?'

In the end, she gave him money which he took with a nod, his face still red from her blow. She called the dog and made her way down the hill by the direct route. By the time she reached the main road she had made up her mind to leave Spain.

It's not because of the donkey, the man with the whip. It's because . . . because, she thought to herself, waiting a full ten minutes before she dared to cross the main road, because everything is wrong. Nothing is right. I'm not right for it, and it's not right for me.

Safe on the other side, she paused, and looked back up the path she had just descended. He *had* been beating the animal. Unmercifully. Just the same, she had attacked some-one.

Back at the pueblo, drinking tea in her sitting-room, Mrs Frampton pondered for a long time. She sat, almost motionless, for an hour, rising only to make a fresh pot of tea, to fetch more hot water. She poured a last cup, then allowed it to get cold. And rose suddenly and went to the bookcase for an atlas. Turning the pages on her lap, she stopped, and looked up at the wall. It was odd. She felt in a sort of stupor. Empty. Without feeling, without pain, without anything. At the same time, it was plain, it was obvious, that something (though she didn't know what) had happened.

Chapter 5

M RS FRAMPTON PUT down the last of the brochures. The trouble with tours was they never fitted. They weren't what you wanted. They were like the pictures in the fashion magazines: you wanted the sleeves from this dress, the skirt from that. If the fabric was right, the cut was silly, if the cut was generous and pleasing, the skirt was up over the knees and the fabric was gold lurex. How often had she thrown down the glossies at the hairdresser's! Where was the skill in dressing size-eight nineteen year olds? They looked good in grain-sacks! What heathen woman-hater made tiny waists and thigh-length skirts the fashion? Anyway, they were cutting their own throats since vast numbers of women just stopped buying. We've plenty in the wardrobe to fall back on, she thought grimly. They ought to remember who's got the longest purse. Still, not surprising they weren't interested in dressing older women. I'd probably be the same. No, I wouldn't.

Her mind wandered to portraits in galleries of old men, old women dignified and handsome in gorgeous robes, solemnly splendid or full of comely simplicity in bonnets, in decorous redingotes, panniers or farthingales. She looked down at a glistening brochure illustration of two grinning grandmothers in a gondola and pushed it away with a grunt. What was the point of taking a tour? If you refused to go in for all the scheduled activities it was a waste of money; if you did, you were likely to end up comatose and bored silly with ruins, grating guides and unselected fellow voyagers. Either you were hurtled through ten days of gawping and indigestion or you were lumbered off to places whose only point seemed to be their need for tourism and the prosperity promised by invasion. She turned a page.

Look at that – half a day's toiling up a Turkish mountain to

26

see an icon of Saint John . . . 'illustration half-size' . . . in an 1860 ruined chapel, donkeys provided. Yes, and we know who the donkeys are, thought Mrs Frampton nastily.

A shriek of laughter shot through her open sitting-room window like a guided missile. Mrs Frampton looked up. There they were. As usual. The permanent fixtures, Long John Eliette, Simonette of the newly-acquired pearl-pink rinse and Henriette, the daft one, in a frilly yellow beach dress . . . all clustered at 'their' table by the pool, the only one shaded by the stone pine. Daftie was wearing daisy-petal sunglasses and looked, with her long nose, like an anteater. Mrs Frampton pulled a face.

How can they sit there, within sight of my window? Do they think I've forgotten? That because I give them the time of day it's over – it doesn't matter that the shrieking Daftie, now playing silly buggers with someone else's beach ball, ran off with Vic, and that five days later he was as dead as a pork chop on a platter?

You never loved him, said a small voice from within. It was thirty years of misery. Still. Suppose I'd been keen, would that have stopped her? No. Not for the first time Mrs Frampton wondered if the other two had put her up to it. Likely. They would have colluded, with mindless spite.

You're bad news, she thought, craning towards the window, hoping to see Daftie fall in. I'm right. It was time to go, to leave the beautiful, damaged province of Málaga.

She would sell her house with the pale voile curtains, the Moroccan archway, and the garden . . . oh, the garden! How could she abandon the pink and golden shower of bougainvillaea, the drooping yellow muscat vine, Vic's strawberry bed, the old olive tree? What about the lily pots, her double pink hibiscus? The Madame Alfred Carrière rose which reared in high elegance over the sea wall, gift and precious memory of Little May . . .?

'Oh, bugger it.'

Mrs Frampton, speaking aloud, struggled to her feet, sending brochures flying. Taking her hat and sunshade, she went out of the side gate and across the terrace to the Frenchwomen.

'May – comment ça va?'

'How arr yoo?'

'Bonjour, madame.'

She squinted at them all, head cocked.

'What are you lot up to – assassination?

Eliette, uncomprehending but suspecting raillery, looked down her nose. Simonette, assuming a compliment, simpered. Daftie, as always, looked away, from time to time darting coy little glances at Mrs Frampton like a loved child expecting, through its natural charm, forgiveness for small demeanour.

Mrs Frampton, inured to this graceless display, ignored the woman. She waved a hand to summon José and ordered a *cappuccino*.

'How is the weight progressing?'

'Not too well.'

A silence descended on the group. Her presence was unexpected and Mrs Frampton was well aware that she had interrupted a good and no doubt malicious gossip. The Frenchies were merciless if inaccurate mimics. They had a facility for taking off mannerism. They diminished those around them, after which they would smirk, making silly noises through their noses, honking and braying and throwing up their bony fingers like a coven. Mrs Frampton, glancing at the three in turn from behind the safety of her sunglasses, felt a sudden strong pang of release, as of a knot inside unravelling.

'I'm leaving.'

'Quoi?'

'I'm selling up. Selling my house. Leaving the pueblo.'

The Frenchies, after exchanging glances, broke into rapid torrents of Gallic hissing. Then, galvanically, they reverted to English and began to interrogate her with intense and urgent concentration.

Oh, I am a fool, thought Mrs Frampton, at first misled into a belief that their urgency implied regret at the prospect of her departure. The truth emerged soon enough.

What sum, *par exemple*, was she thinking of asking for her property? She must comprehend that the house would be to the convenience of few prospective purchasers. The third bedroom was *follement* small, with a back outlook. The dwelling was situated at the far end of the pueblo, not so convenient for the main entrance or the office, let alone the shop . . . one had to traverse two terraces, possibly in the rain. A doctor, for example, should such an unhappy crisis arrive . . . one would prefer not to think of it.

Mrs Frampton, watching billowing spinnakers in the bay, listened to their rapid fusillades with sardonic humour. They were certainly scattering the target.

They must have had their eye on my place for ages.

A sickening thought occurred. Suppose it was Daftie who wanted it? Her mind flickered on the vision of Daftie sitting in her living-room, putting up brocade curtains and filling the rooms with triangular chrome tables and map lampshades with puce trim. Outrage filled the stomach. She let them run on, nodding submissively as they grumbled about the largeness of the garden, the threat of further development across the stream where an Arab official dwelt in palatial serenity, until, inevitably, the subject of price arose.

'I shan't be asking a high price,' said Mrs Frampton comfortably, putting down her cup and wiping the froth from her mouth with one of Gudrun's drawn-thread handkerchiefs. 'As a matter of fact, I've already had an offer.'

'Already? You have an offer?'

Lofty's voice was a bat squeak. So *she* was the one who wanted it!

'Yes, but it wasn't serious. Much too low.'

A panting silence reigned. She kept them waiting.

'A friend of mine. He's short of cash so it was a hopeless offer. Two hundred and fifty thousand.'

Baffled looks were exchanged.

'Pounds. English pounds. I'm not sure what that is in Spanish.'

Work that out, she thought. And sat back, watching their faces. It was a treat. Shocked outrage, baulked fury, were chased by trembling underlips and gradual, breathless smiles. Never mind that the price mentioned was way beyond the financial capacities of any one of the three. No. What began to create a festive climate around the table was the corollary of Mrs Frampton's information. An offer of twenty million pesetas? Regarded as too low? Why, that made their own houses worth . . .

She allowed the dreams of financial glory to swill back and forth before laughing out loud and confessing that she had been joking. This caused total confusion. Joking? About money? Baleful frowns demanded explication that was impossible to supply.

Mrs Frampton, taking pity, solved the impasse by ordering tapas and white wine all round, and a congenial atmosphere was restored. Her house, at the quiet, private end of the pueblo, had always been the most coveted.

They can't wait, she thought, watching the forks prod into the baby squids, the small, pungent sausages. Any moment now they'll be telling me how much I can save on agent's commission by a private sale.

Sure enough, with the precision of a green mamba, Lanky stepped in with a murmured offer. And amazingly, or not so amazingly, paid for Mrs Frampton's post-prandial coffee, before repeating her offer in more concrete terms, leaning across the table with an intimate smile not an inch from Mrs Frampton's nose.

In the end, the matter was nicely resolved. Luis and Gudrun, returning from Sweden, bought the house from her. Luis gave up his poky quarters over the restaurant, and Gudrun sold her house at the back of the pueblo to a German belly dancer who slept all day so was not deprived by the lack of a sea view. Mrs Frampton, baulked in her attempt to give all her furniture to the newlyweds, allowed them to pay her a modest sum for some pieces and sold the rest at auction. The mementoes and linen, her water-colours and half-finished oils, were put into dry store with Emilio as guardian. When Mrs Frampton asked him for his fee for this, he merely patted her hand.

How I'm going to miss them, she thought – these country ways. I'm giving it up, as if it were nothing, as if it had taken no time, no effort, no bad days, to achieve my life here. I'm giving up my house, my friends, I'm giving up the sun . . . and worse, worst of all, I'm abandoning my post. I am the survivor. The link. One of the creators of Casa John. How can I walk away? Is it really what I want? Does what I want matter? I'm not myself. This isn't the time to make permanent decisions. That is the last thing I should do. What I ought to have done was put everything on hold. For the time being. Why did I say yes at once when Gudrun and Luis asked about the house?

She knew why. It was because of the pressure that the three Frenchwomen had put on her over the weeks. Their antics had sickened her to numbness and then to a dull revenge. She would watch the cabal by the pool jerking their heads over the table as they sought to prise her property from her.

That's why I let Gudrun have it cheap.

Money made her tired. It was everything nowadays . . . money, money, money. People talked of nothing else. You switched on the radio and there were the programmes, in Spanish, in French, even on the World Service. How to get the best deal. How to stack it up. In the clubs the old men and women sat over bridge tables, and, when they weren't trying to grab it off one another, they were talking of the best currency to get into, when to sell punts, pounds, yen, dollars. Everything was identified, confined to its price tag. Countries sold off human services, gas, electricity, water, for maximum profit, selling to the few what had been owned by the many. They'd sell off the air if they could, float shares in the sea if they could figure out a selling campaign.

None of her brooding speculations helped to solve the dilemma, or to lift her from the nowhere in which she found herself. Only one thought dominated, implacably. It was time to go. To get out. Lying in bed at night, trying to find a way forward, only bleakness invaded.

I need Little May!

She tried to invoke that cool presence, ask her advice. Nothing came. She turned and sweated and got up and changed her pillow slip, or the bottom sheet. She made cool drinks and sat by the window, looking out at the moonlight.

It's grief, I suppose.

There were other problems. She began to feel odd when she went out, self-conscious and panicky. Yet indoors she felt stifled, so much so that one night she dragged the big cushions from the sofa and slept on the patio. For a while she took to whisky, but it gave her sour risings and a bad head. In the end, discarding the Italian brochures for want of the energy to choose among them, Mrs Frampton packed her bags, and, with a single brief telephone call to Mother Caterina, took the train to Madrid.

'Where will you go?'

'I've no idea.'

'The Blessed Virgin go with you.'

In Madrid, Honoré was recovering from the latest repair to his face. His eyes, dark, looked up without recognition at first, and his speech, from the painkilling drugs, was slow and hesitant. She sat and talked to him brightly, telling him the news. There was little response. Now and then he murmured, and when she rose to go he turned his head fractionally towards her.

'I'm going away for a while, Honoré.'

His dark eyes looked up at her, the lashes long and dark and straight. She groaned to herself. He had been such a handsome man, with his fine shoulders and long legs. On one visit, during a nurse's check, she had noticed his feet, undamaged in the fire. They were so beautiful that she wanted to draw them, make a crayon sketch of the high arch, the perfect heel.

'I'll write. Don't worry, they're doing wonders for you here.' She took his hand. It was inert. 'If you need me, I'll come back. Get the nurse to write a letter for you. I'll let you know where I am.'

She consulted his doctors, asked to see the senior consultant. There was an Italian surgeon, famous in such cases. Though, said the consultant, the patient was not co-operative. He showed Mrs Frampton photographs of the mutilated shoulder, the seared chest, the horrible, damaged area on the right side of the face and head.

'As you see, he was trying to rescue his employer.' On the hand, burned deep, was the mark of the car door where Honoré had wrenched and wrenched despairingly.

'The Italian surgeon . . . what will it cost?'

Mrs Frampton wrote out a cheque and signed a guarantee of further reimbursements where required. Then she asked to use the telephone and booked a flight to London. From there she hired a car and drove west to her daughter Chloe.

Chapter 6

C HLOE AND PATRICK, with their children's education in mind, had settled in the West Country, on the outskirts of Bristol. They spoke of being close to a centre of excellence, a phrase which obscurely offended Mrs Frampton, but she forgave them. So many words seemed to grate these days . . . toilet, with its pinched ring, like the jokes about women who put on their gloves to have sex. And heritage, which seemed to be everywhere.

Why don't they turn the whole bloody country into a museum and have done with it! It's going backwards to Christmas, any road.

The public clocks had long ceased to work, the water in Cornwall was coming poisoned out of the taps, her old friend Phil had been waiting two years for a hip replacement and was lurching about on crutches – Phil, who had been the best jitterbugger in the village. And what was post-feminism? What was that supposed to mean? That women had stopped supporting one another?

In Mrs Frampton's lifetime the outlook for women had improved beyond measure, mostly through better medicine. Mothers and babies no longer died from the awful ailments she remembered from her childhood, women bleeding to death, collapsing from infection, underweight babies in cold, damp houses turning blue in their mothers' arms. Or dying from measles or diptheria, or typhoid. Or TB, or polio.

In our days we didn't have hot water, central heating, electric lights, nor launderettes and dry cleaning. It was fill up the copper of a Monday, boil all day, heave out the sheets with the copper stick, out on the line if you were lucky with the weather, if not, all over the house. Then the ironing, and the mending – the mending! Darn, darn, darn, turn the sheets and frayed collars and cuffs, unpick old jumpers for socks, patch shoes with bits of rubber.

They don't know they're born. We worked! All the time! When I wasn't helping Mum with the logs, or skinning rabbits, or plucking boiling fowls, it was the garden. You grew a lot of what you ate. That was the cheapest way. When the crop was finished you harvested the seed, swopped with your neighbour. You bottled fruit, dried apple rings, made jam from woodland brambles. Nothing was wasted. Every brown paper bag, every nail, every tack, was hoarded. One old woman even had a box marked 'Bent Nails'. You never knew when something would come in. You had to improvise. When the outside world intervened it was usually disaster – authorities to kick you out of your home, the landlord to up the rent, the undertaker to haul you away. Otherwise, you were on your own. Your job was to shut up, mind your manners before your betters, or else.

She remembered Uncle Bill who'd been an undergardener at the big house and ducked off the end of the line into a bush when Queen Mary came, rather than bow the neck to the old girl. And been sacked for it. All those men, the survivors of the 'Great' War. Pity the Americans had come in, it would have ended sooner without them. Without that vicious Versailles, who knows, Dad had said, with more of a compromise, perhaps the second war needn't have happened. But then, who was her Dad? He wasn't supposed to know anything. Just a labourer with bad lungs because he'd been gassed. No education. What could he know? A man like that must be an idiot, fit for nothing.

Mrs Frampton, sitting on the grassy slope at the back of Chloe's farmhouse, turned to her daughter.

'So what does it mean, then, post-feminism?'

'It means that despite the Equal Pay and Sex Discrimination Acts society hasn't moved one inch towards women, the family, that is, the needs of parents and children. So the only way women *can* join is by getting on the conveyor belt, the rat race. Women are drinking more nowadays, getting more heart attacks.'

'More fools them.'

Chloe looked at her mother.

'You're getting a real crease between your eyes.'

'Old age.'

'It makes you look bad-tempered, Mum.'

Chloe had been involved in television journalism. She described the fearsome competition, the chicaneries and back-stabbing, the tensions and anxieties.

'It sounds awful.'

'It was, I resigned.'

'Good for you.'

'Yes, well, I had the option, with Patrick's salary, the money from Dad and the bits you keep sending me, you old – ' She kissed her mother on the cheek and rolled over on the grass. 'I'm privileged. A kept woman.' She sat up, brushing grass from her hair. 'No. What really stuck in the craw was working six months on a piece about Arab women, then having an inept director . . . the woman producer's girlfriend, wished on me. When I kicked up a fuss I was accused of being unsisterly. That broke the heart – hearing feminism invoked for nasty, old-fashioned face-treading. That did it.'

Her face, moody, for a second reminded Mrs Frampton of Vic, and she laughed. And regaled Chloe with the increasing antics of the French trio in the pueblo when they felt Numero Uno, Calle Favoridad slipping from their grasp.

'You're going to miss them.'

'No I'm not.'

'What are you going to do now?'

'Haven't the faintest idea.'

To hide her face Mrs Frampton bent down to pick up young Tom who was caught by his red braces round the stump of an alder tree.

'These things are dangerous.'

'He's all right.' Chloe was in the seventh month of pregnancy, the docile period. Adela, the sturdy three year old, seeing Tom at his grandmother's skirt, clouted him heavily with a wooden boomerang and watched with a cross smile as he was consoled.

Mrs Frampton, despite the ease that watching her grandchildren invoked, began to feel tired at Chloe's after a week. Patrick was on assignment in Turkey, and Chloe's live-in help, Joanna, had a four-year-old boy of her own, who added to the decibels. The house, an old farmhouse, which Chloe had left untouched except for central heating, was restful, low-ceilinged and uneven-floored, muddled in plan, with a room at the back where the children played when it rained. It ought to suit me, thought Mrs Frampton, looking at the old pump outside, wandering round the broken-down stables and yard, watching the wind in the poplar trees. But she felt uneasy: not at home, except when one of the children was on her lap, clawing at her beads or wriggling to get down.

The atmosphere in the house was too modern. Twice within the week, since Chloe's main room was large, there were meetings with other women to discuss campaigns – the need for a local crèche, a pamphlet against a new road, support for disadvantaged children in the borough. The energy of the women, and their commitment, a favourite word, was admirable. But unloving. There was a great deal of blaming. Even more startling was the man-hating, expressed with such force that Mrs Frampton was stirred into stammering interjection, on one occasion disguising her alarm as a point of information query. Cordially invited to sit in, she stationed herself by the kitchen door and made herself useful dispensing sandwiches and clearing dirty cups until requested not to wait on people. The rules were baffling, and hard to work out. She listened in silence as woman after woman reported new affront, read extracts from newspapers. Men, it seemed, were the cause of all the ills. They were violent, they killed people, they attacked and raped women, they abused children. Men had the power. And misused it. Women, the elderly, and the children of the world did not commit violence. And had no power, were not in possession of the riches of the world.

It makes you think, mused Mrs Frampton, putting in her curlers in her bedroom. Still. Fair's fair. Men have done some good things. You can't blame them because women didn't feature in the past – poor things, how could they, being pregnant all the time, or ill with something to do with their wombs. It was a fact of nature.

Asked to contribute at meeting number two she made anodyne
remarks and sensed the women dismiss her as an oldie from an
unliberated past. It wasn't true, but they seemed more comfortable
viewing her this way. They condescended, and were protective,
treating her as though she were mildly handicapped. The trouble
is, she thought, sluicing off the plates and putting the leftovers
in the bucket for the ducks, they don't know they're born.
Everybody's wrong but them. Find a scapegoat. Them and
us. Long ago, Mrs Frampton had discovered the uselessness
of that. It was no use blaming *them* . . . even when they were
guilty, the predators. It wasted energy. You had to realise there
was no *them* and *us*. That there was only *us*. Somehow that got
you up off the ground. She tried to say some of this and there
was a thoughtful silence when she finished and a lone woman
clapped.

After they left and the last car door had banged, she sat in the
garden alone. Well, they were having a go, the girls. Trying
to make things better for themselves and their children. And
times were different . . . the problems were different. Time
itself seemed to have speeded up. Everywhere you looked there
was pressure.

The next morning she said to Chloe over coffee, 'I think I'll go
to Paris. There's an exhibition of paintings by Degas.'

Chloe looked up and Mrs Frampton could tell she was pleased.

She thinks it's a good sign, that I'm starting to pull out of
it.

'Would you like me to come with you?'

'Do you want to?'

'Yes, love it.'

Mrs Frampton was not fooled by the bright tone.

'No. You're better off here taking it easy. You don't want to go
plodding about Paris; anyway, Pat will be home next week.'

'Where will you stay?'

'Somewhere nice, I think.'

Yes, why not? She remembered a conversation in Marbella
and rang L'Hôtel, on the Left Bank, and booked a suite in her
halting French. Oscar Wilde had lived there, and lanky Eliette,

enthusing over a one-night stay, had recommended the hotel to Mrs Frampton, at the same time doubting her capacity to afford such recherché magnificence. Unless, she had simpered, dear Madame Liu had blessed Madame Frampton with a good munificence in her will. Mrs Frampton, who had kept the details of her own inheritance on the death of her husband very quiet, allowing her modest life-style to mislead, had been equally reticent on the matter of May's estate. It was public knowledge that the bulk of her fortune had gone to charitable foundations created in the names of her husband and children. Cinthia had been well taken care of at the time of her betrothal and was married to a rich man. John's family were amply provided for and Little May's bequests to friends had been made with exquisite thoughtfulness.

Mrs Frampton herself had received a small Corot and a Boudin landscape that she had once copied, trying to understand the brushwork, with Little May at her elbow. To her surprise, she was also left the Matisse of the woman at the window, as well as May's string of pearls and a simple gold bangle engraved with a dog's head that Little May had worn a good deal. Now it sat on Mrs Frampton's arm, fitting snugly rather than loosely as on its previous owner. At first she had shuddered to see it and, coming across it one day among her handkerchiefs, had backed away from the glint in horror. But the day she left Spain she put it on without thinking, and now rarely went out without it.

Chapter 7

H ER SUITE AT L'Hôtel was in the Empire style with armchairs deeply upholstered in blue and crimson. Sitting by
the open window which looked into an open courtyard, Mrs
Frampton, a tea-tray before her, felt an unfamiliar sense of
relaxation. There had been several threatened panics, moments
when it seemed she was not going to be able to leave the
haven of her daughter's house. She had confided in Chloe,
who had taken her to a woman doctor. Who had instructed
her in deep breathing, in coasting through panic attacks. And
advised self-rewards and cosseting. Mrs Frampton had taken a
seasickness pill on the day of departure to relax herself, hired
a car to the airport, and travelled first class. Walking into the
mellow, inviting suite, she felt guilty. What a waste, just for
her. She should have brought Chloe for a rest from the children
and some shopping.

No. She's better where she is, in the garden.

Honesty, too, prevailing, made her nod with a faint smile.
She was better on her own. The time in Bristol, now it was
over, could be savoured and cherished. Adela and Tom were
miracles, shining, quick and new. But noisy and messy . . .
she had forgotten what a mess infants made. Used to the full
staffing at Casa John, Mrs Frampton only now recalled the
energy needed to pick up after children, even more to make
them pick up after themselves.

She had never been very tidy with Mike and Chloe. There
had been the reaction, in those days, from the pre-war Truby
King years, when babies, you were told, had to be fed every
four hours, and not messed about with in between. She smiled,
remembering days on the wards trying to persuade women to
breast-feed their babies, to change fashion back from the bottle.

And she dwelt briefly on those years, those grey Fifties. And reading about strontium ninety and caesium, up there in the atmosphere, falling on her children. And trying to get HIM, Vic, to sign the Ban-the-Bomb form, without success.

'What's it got to do with me?' had been his answer. What had anything been to do with him, apart from his business, and his standing at the local chamber of commerce, at the Rotary Club. She grimaced, remembering the long-drawn-out row over her two nights a week at the local art class. Why waste her time on drawing – it had baffled him.

So many battles, most of the domestic ones lost. Staying alive, inside, had been the challenge. Now, in retrospect, it seemed puzzling. Why hadn't she left him at the beginning, after the first dismal year? Before the children . . . or even after? She could have managed somehow, with part-time nursing.

You know why, don't you? You thought you couldn't get another man. You thought you were ugly.

Looking at old photographs, she learned, too late, that she had not been ugly. Her face as a girl had been pretty, her eyes large and laughing. Her legs had never been marvellous, but her waist had been tiny and her bosom lovely. Except that when it was truly lovely, when she was in her teens, no one had ever seen it but herself.

What a shame. I should have taken a picture. But if I had I'd never have had the nerve to get it developed.

She remembered an argument with Chloe and her friends about beauty contests. For once roused, and unafraid of their cool eyes, she had argued that the girls were sneered at because they were working class, for their hair, choice of gown, their nervous attempts at conversation with some slick interviewer. What was wrong with looking at young, beautiful people? she had asked. I've always liked looking at beauty, it makes your heart ache, it doesn't last. There had been a silence. We don't celebrate anything, she had said. Where I've been, in Spain, people still do. Yes, Mariolatry, someone had muttered, and Mrs Frampton had remembered the wooden, painted statues of the Virgin in the Holy Week parades with inward pain that was mixed up with Little May. She had changed the subject and said it was probably something to do with sunshine and taking your clothes off, that puritanism seemed to be a band running round the earth at a sunless latitude. And the women had looked at her with brief interest.

Whether she should have left Vic, or stayed – what was the difference now? Slowly it seemed that now the need for peace and quiet, for time to herself, was paramount.

I'm not myself. In any case, myself isn't twenty-four any more, however silly I feel inside sometimes. Whether I like it or not I'm getting older. I must cut my cloth.

She looked out at the pigeons on the grey mansard roof, at the lace curtains blowing from a casement across the courtyard. The women at Chloe's remained in her mind. She smelt again someone's rose scent, chocolate biscuits melting in the sun, as the women sprawled on the grass, hair loose, legs brown, their feet bare, toes without corns, unbent by the crippling narrow shoes of their mothers and grandmothers. They *were* different. A new breed. She felt the weight of their awesome energy, their sense of purpose. And their intransigent hostilities. But perhaps fighting, their own sex half the time, perhaps, after all, it was a necessary part of progress. Perhaps it was right. They were good girls, fine women. Thinking, questioning, courageous, demanding equal partnership, a voice.

It was just . . . what was it? It was that they were pagan. There seemed to be no consciousness of virtue. Of vice. Oh, in the old days, didn't we hate trudging off to Sunday School every Sunday, and choir practice twice a week. And sitting through endless sermons which made no sense half the time . . . with words like manna, hallelujah and the begats, all mystifying, about people who had nothing to do with damp England. And religion caused wars. Still, people went to war about most things, anything. At least with a religious teaching you got a grounding in goodness. You were made aware – not to be nasty to your neighbour, to treat others as you would want to be treated.

The whole idea of it – God is Love – had struck Mrs Frampton early on as an amazing notion when you thought about it. When it was clear to most people that the way up was to conquer and dominate. Jesus must have been spectacular. An idea of such wetness – such a feminine idea – appealing to all those tough Roman emperors was stunning. Had Christianity led to the notions of courtly love and decency towards women, the notion of tenderness, which followed? Why must they be so harsh, those girls? Their reports of rapes, of attacks, were distressing and alarming. *Was* it getting worse? Or was it being noticed more, resisted? Who could say? Was honour towards women being discarded? Were the attacks because women were daring to break the rules, come out of purdah and demand their share of the light? Was resentment breaking down the old code? Was it because women seemed to be spurning protection that men were turning on them, savagely showing them who was boss? Where was the hate coming from? Who was to blame?

In many ways, ordinary working men were worse off than women. Machines had taken over their traditional roles, from the industrial revolution on. Brains, not brawn, were needed for the maintenance and manipulation of modern gadgetry. Strength and courage, traditional male sources of pride, were humbled. The Luddites were on to something. Now, more and more, machines were evicting men from heavy industry. They were going on strike to be allowed to go on burrowing underground, to sweat in smelting yards. Firms nowadays demanded skills that were traditionally female . . . literacy, quick-wittedness, fine-fingered ingenuity, a talent for persuasion. Women, programmed in complaisance to keep the rope from their backs, were proving adept at selling, at public relations. No wonder men felt threatened.

Mrs Frampton lay back in her comfortable *bergère*, lulled by the cooing of the pigeons. What could she have said to those shining girls, with their straight teeth and limbs, that would not have seemed old hat? She knew what she had wanted to say. Shut up, the lot of you, spoiled brats. You're privileged, princesses, compared with us, and with most women in the world. You're lucky, all of you. And yet. Somewhere she was in the wrong of it. True, they had new freedoms, new opportunities – better food, living quarters, instant light and heat, cars, cheap holidays. But against that – oh, the crush, the rush and tear of it. We were so much slower. Everything was face to face, quarrels, friendships. And your fears were there in front of you, your worries defined. It was a matter of physical survival. Now everything's gone intangible. When she had tried to rescind her order for the sewing kit, the man on the telephone had said it was too late. The order was on the computer. She looked at her watch and got up to change for dinner.

Oh, stop worrying about them!

People will get fed up with the rat race; there was already a move back to nature and organic husbandry. Hedgerows were being planted again, women weren't wearing fur coats any more, there was a fear for the planet itself. The fights were still on, but the ground was different. Different battles. Different tactics.

If only they weren't so militant. To abandon affection, even forgiveness, was that the only way? Mrs Frampton sat down suddenly, finding herself weeping, and without a handkerchief or tissue to hand.

Now what's the matter with me!

She knew what the matter was. These girls had left her behind. Chloe and Pat and the babies had their own lives to live.

I don't have anyone to be affectionate, to be intimate with . . . I'm not first with anyone any more.

It looked as if she was going to have to learn to put up with it.

Chapter 8

THE STREETS OF Paris were cold, and the wind trying. After the unseasonably warm weather of the English West Country, Mrs Frampton felt chilled, and quickened her step. She had gone out firmly immediately after her breakfast tray. On the bridge, panic had threatened, but she had taken deep breaths and walked on with bolder strides. There would be none of that. Near to the further side of the bridge she paused and looked over the parapet at the water, full and yellow, swirling past the piers with dangerous strength. For a moment she was compelled. There was fear, then an almost sensuous weakness, and she leaned further towards the water.

No! For a fraction of a second, in terrible need, she invoked Little May. Help me!

But the thought of May set off inner feelings of such pain, such knife-loss, that, her face wet with immediate, copious tears, she set off again grimly, clutching her umbrella and bag. On the Île de la Cité, consulting her guide, she looked for a famous old coffee shop. It was gone, replaced by a smart shop-front. She turned north, and walked along the rue de Rivoli, and then north again until, her mouth dry, she collapsed into a broad basket chair on a café pavement.

Her mood relaxed. A woman in a red suit went by, leaving a trail of metallic hyacinth. Diorissimo. Mrs Frampton, enjoying the rare forbidden pleasure of real coffee, slumped back, grinning at a schoolboy weighed down by his satchel who blew a large bubble of gum at her and ran. A tiny man with a tiny dog tottered by. Both of them wore identical tartan macs – now that *was* silly. She watched the pair hop fastidiously across the road, the man imperious, the dog skittering in alarm. The traffic thinned to a lull and for a moment the street was so quiet that she could hear the assertive trills of the starlings in the plane trees. Then a surge of cars hurtled forward, destroying thought.

An old woman approached, moving from table to table, displaying flowers. Mrs Frampton leaned forward as the woman drew close. Could they be . . .? surely not – they were *Magnolia campbellis*! The empress of flowers – huge, pale-pink chalices on grey-branched stems! Where on earth had they come from? The old woman, seeing Mrs Frampton's gaze, thrust the flowers under her nose. Yes . . . that was it . . . the strange smell, a mixture of chamois leather and crystallised violets.

You old vandal, thought Mrs Frampton. You've ripped those off a tree growing over a wall . . . you've dodged into an open gateway and wrenched down a whole bough. *Campbellis* took twenty years to come into bloom. Not a tree to plant in late middle age. And they won't last in water!

Just to gaze at them was worth the money. She took out twenty francs. The old woman took the money and scuttled off across the square. Mrs Frampton, sipping her coffee, gazed at the three pale globes propped up before her. A cab drew up and disgorged young women. She hailed it and threw down the money for her drink.

I'll go to the exhibition now. I'll tell him to take me to the Grand Palais.

However, seated inside she leaned forward and said, 'Cimetière Père Lachaise, s'il vous plaît.'

The vast cemetery was tiring. Mrs Frampton bought a map which indicated the tombs of the renowned and sat on a seat trying to map a route for herself. Chopin was a long way from Simone Signoret, the grave of Callas was nowhere near Verdi. She began to stroll and somewhere along the uneven cobbles she lost the map. The wind had dropped and despite the cold day she began to perspire.

I'll go to the top of the rise. Perhaps, on high ground, she could get her bearings.

She carried the magnolias carefully. She would separate the blossoms, to be left in homage on the graves of the mighty. Her legs began to give out. One bower of unexpected colour turned out to be the tomb of Edith Piaf. She laid a flower among the

45

profusion, reading the name of the young husband, killed in a car crash, and buried with his wife. She walked on, past magnificent new granite tombs, Chinese or Vietnamese, strange neighbours for the sparrow. She felt odd, calm, at home among the dear loved ones of the past. The roar of traffic was no more than a hum and there was no other sound but the murmur of branches above and, once, the rusty trill of a robin.

Somewhere within her a forbidden door opened. She sat down, on a worn old tomb. And allowed in the fearful. The little coffin in the shadowy crypt in Spain, lying on the tomb which already held the remains of John Liu . . . she could see every detail in her mind, smell the suffocating scent of the lilies, the dusty aroma of the priest's cassock, the incense, even the alum in her new handkerchief. She had not wept but her nose had run continuously through the ceremony and the handkerchief had been drenched.

I should have stayed, I should never have come away.

She sat, motionless, twisting the branch of flowers slightly.

What do you want, May?

There seemed to be an answering surge of sound from the trees above, so prompt that Mrs Frampton smiled. She gazed at the blooms in her hand and said aloud, 'Where shall I put these? You choose.'

An elderly woman, approaching silently behind her, moved aside in passing, startled at Mrs Frampton's ringing tone. Mrs Frampton smiled in apology.

'Pardon, Madame.'

The woman smiled back and lifted a black glove. Mrs Frampton rose and walked on.

I'll just walk anywhere.

She turned left and then right and followed a long path to a knoll, then made a slight descent past a thicket of yellow privet. Now she could see an exit gate. She made towards it.

I've had enough. I don't know what I'm doing here.

As she reached the gate the woman in the lodge house, who had been cleaning the windows, turned with her basin of washing water and threw it on the tarmac. Her eyes flickered at the flowers, and Mrs Frampton, noting the woman's softening gaze, realised she was still carrying the magnolias. She smiled and held them out to the woman who nodded thanks, eyes wide at the enormous blossoms.

The Grand Palais was crowded. You had to queue for each picture, edge in using your elbows as old ladies barged in front, students craned, matrons smelling of Femme and Jolie Madame caught you in the ribs with sharp-angled handbags. Mrs Frampton had entered, after waiting her turn outside for thirty minutes, with the special expectation particular to viewing pictures, a mixed feeling of belonging, of cherishing, of wanting and needing to learn, of feeling remorseless in judgement and yearning to worship all at once. She soon became disillusioned.

I shouldn't have wasted my legs at the cemetery.

Was it tiredness? Her general state of derangement? Or were many of these paintings very bad? She pushed past groups of people reading a huge précis of the painter's life which was stuck on a wall and moved into a larger salon.

What a lot of old rubbishy work!

Mrs Frampton, primed by her discussions with Chloe and her friends, was not inclined to breathe over the endless paintings of female flesh. They were salacious, sloppy, not well observed . . . she remembered the love and truth and honesty of a Lucian Freud drawing in Chloe's bedroom . . . couldn't Degas see? She walked through the last room quickly, pausing only before a beautiful and energetic painting of horses and jockeys and a small, rare still life. In the foyer she turned over the pages of highly priced coffee books. Yes, here were the good paintings . . . aha, she had been right! The old boy had gone off, his sight had worsened as he aged. Whoever had chosen and hung this sloppy, disappointing exhibition had liked or been stuck with only the bad canvases.

Just the same, the girls were right. Most of these women were painted as objects, creatures of subjection, at best, icons.

Now, there's something. I came away from Chloe's so ratty at all their moaning and now it seems I'm . . . what?

She stood on the steps, putting up her umbrella against the drizzling rain, and moved off, trying to hail a taxi without success. She walked and then, exhausted, stopped for a bowl of soup. Which made her sleepy.

I suppose I could go to the pictures.

But she was tired. By marching firmly into the middle of the street she flagged down a taxi. That evening she stayed in bed, too weary to go down to the dining-room, even to ring for room service. The next morning she woke with a temperature. For five days she sweated in bed, helped by the gentle ministrations of the young doctor called in by the solicitous management. On the sixth day he pronounced her temperature down to one point above normal.

'You recover, Madame.'

'I don't feel like it.'

The young man gave her an imperious glance and rose from his perch at the end of her handsomely appointed bed. He picked up his bag and continued to look down at Mrs Frampton. She felt low, and even lower with her hair not done, in her nightie which needed a wash, before the young flower of Gaul tapping a lordly finger on his sternum.

'You are here alone?'

Well, that was obvious. She had told him that she was widowed.

'You have no friends, relations?'

'Yes, but not with me.'

'You prefer to travel alone.'

For some reason, she was unable to answer him, and turned her head away. He went on talking as she looked out at the grey roofs across the courtyard.

'You must attend to yourself, Madame. You are reaching the age when living becomes a matter of decision.'

That was perceptive of him. She looked him in the face, and for the first time saw his intelligence. She had been misled by the beautiful curl of the top lip, the calves in the pale-grey trousers.

'That's very bright of you.'

'We don't speak of me.'

'What do you suggest?'

'First, go south, where it is warm.'

'South?'

But he was writing on his pad.

'Here is the address of a very good hotel. Behind Cannes. Excellent food, quiet, fine views of the sea, and beautiful gardens. Here.' She took the piece of paper unwillingly and, looking up briefly, caught a smile on his face.

'I think you are willing enough to help others, Madame . . .' (She had told him of her nursing background.) 'But not yourself. This is either arrogance, or you do not care enough, do not believe yourself worthy. As my patient I ask you to believe.'

There was silence. She made to put the paper on the bedside table.

'I do not,' he said, 'give such an address to all my patients.'

She looked up.

'Why to me?'

The young doctor paused, one arm in his coat, for a second disconcerted.

'You need the sun, Madame.' He smiled a delicious smile which changed his face completely. 'You remind me of my favourite aunt. Who is, just the same, also wilful.' Doing up his coat, he shrugged in the inimitable French way. 'Because . . . what have you to lose?'

Chapter 9

MRS FRAMPTON TOOK her seat at the café with the good coffee and watched the people. It was amazing. She had breakfasted as usual at nine and then walked along for the English paper and her small coffee. Here they were, the French Mesdames, on their way to the market, their hair perfectly coiffed, white piqué collars gleaming, hems straight, shoes shining, all of them ready for a photocall, for a visit from the President of France. Mrs Frampton lifted her face to the sun. Yes, she had been right.

After three weeks in the upholstered arms of the doctor's hotel, she had escaped west to Bandol. The perfection of the first hotel, like the women passing before her, had at first been nourishing, like a blanket bath, a body massage, a Devonshire cream tea. But then the *petits soins* had begun to get on her nerves. The endless discussions about food: were the mange-touts absolutely *à point*, was the *brandade de morue* as well made as that eaten at Aix? Her mind had begun to spin. You had to keep up all the time. She found herself messing about with scarves, putting on and taking off brooches before going in to dinner. You felt the effort was worth it since the French noticed everything. That was the trouble. There were days when you wanted to scuff about in slippers, eat in an old cardigan. She had begun to fall behind, miss meals because she had cancelled her hot hour at the Cannes hairdresser's. One morning she heard herself give notice of departure. She hired a car and driver and drove to Saint-Tropez, quiet out of season, then to Sanary, and Bandol. Where the hotel was both relaxed and large enough for her to lose herself, where she could watch the other guests and their children without anyone taking the slightest notice of her. Where the staff were cordial but unobtrusive, a merry lot who flirted with one another in the dining-room.

She picked up her copy of the local paper and looked idly at the small pictures of houses for sale. One caught her eye. It was a farmhouse in a village above Bandol.

Goodness! That was cheap!

She read the columns, comparing prices.

It must be a ruin.

She took off for her morning promenade and, pausing to cross a side road, noticed a photograph of the same farm in the estate agent's window. For no reason, she went inside. Yes, said the young woman, the farm was indeed for sale. It was old, created of stone, with four bedrooms and a cobbled yard . . . no, there were no gardens to speak of, but a small stream ran through the property, a garden of much beauty could be designed. There was also a small vineyard, tended by a neighbouring farmer, who would be prepared to continue the harmonious and shared arrangement as with Madame Plessis, the elderly owner who wished to sell.

'Why is it so cheap?'

The girl made a moue.

'You will see.' She crossed the room and took down a large key.

'Madame wishes to view?'

'Now?'

'If it is convenient. We are slow at this time of year.'

'Shouldn't you ring the owner?'

The girl shook her head. The owner had no telephone. They would arrive, it would not inconvenience. If Madame Plessis was not at home, they had the key. It would not incommode.

The road was winding and pleasant, and already the wild flowers were out, later than Spain, but much earlier than England. After ten minutes the girl swooped off the main road up a narrow track bordered by willows, down through a ford and up again, past vines on either side, then, with another gut-wrenching swoop, through a wide gate into a broad yard. Adjacent to the gaunt grey house was the open barn, with hay. A few chickens pecked. Mrs

51

Frampton got out stiffly. There was silence, except for the hens, who made quorking noises round them expectantly and moved off when corn was not forthcoming. Mrs Frampton followed the girl around the corner. A very old woman, bent double, with hairs on her face like the drawings of witches, appeared in the broad doorway and smiled up at them.

Inside, the house was primitive. Water came from a well, there was no electric light, though, said the girl, it could be brought with simplicity from the next farm. The main room was big, and oddly grand, with French windows. Mrs Frampton stepped towards them for the view. It was immediately apparent why the house was cheap. Before her, a field of low-pruned vines away, was a huge chalk outcrop. It cast a deep shadow across the vines and hid the view of the sea below entirely.

Oh, what a shame. That was it, then.

She followed the old woman out to the kitchen with its stone sinks, and to the dairy beyond. This made her heart turn with nostalgia, and the rooms upstairs, with their square proportions, and the attics with their sloping roofs, cried out for simple rehabilitation. And then, on the other side of the house, unmentioned in the details, was a small stable yard with a pigeon loft and a clock, and a room over for the stableman. Mrs Frampton looked at the loose boxes with their iron fittings, the manger still intact, and felt the tears at the back of her eyes. The smell of hay was more pungent, more lovely, than the perfume of flowers – oh, to go back, to be home!

But where was home? She followed the old woman and the girl down the slight slope in front of the house to the stream, her mind elsewhere. As they neared the water she saw a wild pansy, and bent to look at the purple-and-yellow face. There were more – good heavens, they were everywhere . . . The ground was a carpet of flowers. Mrs Frampton trod gingerly as the girl smacked her feet into the flowers mindlessly. As they reached the pellucid chalk stream Mrs Frampton looked up and observed that the old woman was watching her avoid the flowers.

She said, in halting French, 'How long, Madame, have you inhabited this house?'

'I was born here.'

The girl explained that Madame was the youngest of a family of two brothers and two sisters, the others all dead.

'None of them married – can you imagine?' grinned the girl (who was pretty), stepping back through the lake of pansies to the house.

Mrs Frampton and the old woman watched her.

'Where will you go?'

'To a house of God.'

Back inside, the girl explained that the old woman was being accepted into a retreat in the hills. Once the house, which had been on the market for three years, was sold.

'Won't they take her, otherwise?'

There was a rapid fire of French. The girl nodded and said, 'It is her wish that the money goes to the nunnery.'

'I'll take the house,' Mrs Frampton heard herself say.

'Quoi?'

'I shall buy this house. For the price that Madame is asking.'

'Thank you,' said the old woman without surprise, and then, with the sudden, happy smile of a girl, she reached down a dusty bottle of Armagnac. Mrs Frampton took the generously filled glass.

Afterwards, the drive down the hill to Bandol was even more wild. Mrs Frampton, her head buzzing and zooming with the brandy, swayed at the girl's side fearlessly.

What on earth . . . whoops . . . what on earth am I up to?

The girl leaned out, shouting insult at a terrified cyclist.

What *have* I done?!

Chapter 10

N OW THERE WAS plenty to think about. The formalities of acquisition were straightforward since Madame Plessis was the sole and outright owner of the farm and hectares. Mrs Frampton, hunched over her modest croissant the morning after the first and fateful visit, could only gasp in wonder at what she had done. Then, there had still been time to change her mind. But she had not done so. Afterwards, she wondered why. She did not want a farm. She had not decided where to live. If anywhere. The farm itself was in a dreadful mess. Nothing by way of upkeep had been done to the place, by the look of it, for four hundred years. Walls were falling down, the barn was full of ancient rubbish . . . bits of harness, carriages and parts of carriages, chairs, shelving, tools and farm equipment, even mouldering baskets of clothes. Where the stream entered her property the flow was dammed to a weir by a large, swollen mattress, an old bicycle and a high, swaying barrier of broken branches. Everything – everything – would need attention. The house inside was swept, but cobwebs draped the ceilings and corners and debris filled the unused rooms. The old woman's sight was poor. Her strength was failing though she scurried among the chickens and cut-up horsemeat for the hideous and mangy dog, Patrice.

'Patrice . . . Patrice!'

The eldritch cry had followed Mrs Frampton and the girl from the estate as they drove away that first day. It became a joke. The girl, Mireille, became more human as she bathed in her success at the achievement of such an effortless sale. By the end of the week she had perfected a merciless imitation of the dog's sideways lope and twitching head.

'Ah, le pauvre méchant!'

'Why?' asked Mrs Frampton, still laughing at the girl's twisting antics. The girl had answered by drawing her finger across her throat. The dog, she said, would be erased, put down. Why? Because Madame would not be permitted to take such a creature to the retreat. Mrs Frampton nodded thoughtfully and the girl had given her a look.

'You will need a dog for protection, Madame. But such a creature – so ugly, so diseased! My sister-in-law breeds very fine Alsatians. If you wish, I will speak to her.'

'Oh, in for a penny,' Mrs Frampton had murmured obscurely.

She took the dog. Removing his ticks, worming him, curing his mange, his hock infections and bad breath, gave her something to do during the formalities of negotiation, and after all, why not? The dog knew his way around. It was easier than training a messy puppy who would chew everything in sight for at least a year. Besides, it made the old woman happy. Mrs Frampton realised soon enough that she had bought La Bastide for two reasons . . . for the incredible, velvet lakes of wild pansies that grew even on the roof . . . and for Madame Plessis. The old woman's eyes were rarely visible because of her arthritis, you saw only the top of her head. But there had been halting conversations. Almost toothless, her moustache as thick as a man's, Madame Plessis none the less made Mrs Frampton feel at home. There was something about her, a simple cunning, something placid, sure. She wasn't a good person, that wasn't required of her. She was a beast of burden. All her life she had worked the fields and stock without question. She had done what was to be done without hurry, and without shirking. There were no signs on the farm of improvement. Nothing had been modified, brought up to date. A galvanised bucket was the most modern artefact on view. Cutlery was old and bone-handled, the blades worn to nothing; the mixing bowls were earthenware, stained and cracked; the sheets made of linen worn translucent, the last remains of an ancestral dowry. Madame Plessis owned nothing. Except the land. Which, with the help of the neighbouring Danguys, was in beautiful heart. Mrs Frampton prowled among the vines, and through the small olive grove. The trees were set wide apart and pruned low and wide, leaving broad swathes. These were planted with rows of globe artichokes, strawberries, blocks of raspberry canes, neat furrows of early potatoes, spinach and beans. One morning she noticed Yvo, the younger Danguy son, throwing something from a sack between the rows. She walked up and asked if it was chemicals. No, he said, blood and bone.

Am I wrong to feel nostalgia for the past? Mrs Frampton, falling for a cover of sweet peas and hazy gypsophila, had bought a glossy house magazine and been jeered at by Chloe on the way home in the car. Over tea they had argued, turning the pages of gracious country living, sumptuous bedrooms and dining-room layouts. They pored over the small ads at the back, still quarrelling.

'Look at this! "The Old Forge . . . Adrian and Camilla Margerison . . . visitors welcome. Let us design your gates." The yuppies are really into it . . . patchwork quilts, fifteen hundred apiece, anal pottery, frescoes to order, you too can have the Borghese gardens in your loo, here we go, more knicker curtains . . .'

They had laughed, and Mrs Frampton had stoutly hung on to her argument: that there was no harm in it.

'Yes there is. It's rubbish.'

'Better they're doing cane furniture than drugs.'

'The two aren't mutually exclusive, Ma.'

'Well, I don't care. There's a lot worse they could do. It's better than war.'

Yes, Chloe had agreed, but had her mother seen the new art galleries springing up everywhere. The yuppie art explosion?

'It's the "in" thing. It's socially OK. Yuppie art – yart, I call it. I'm telling you, much better when the artist was outside, unacceptable. When they were seen to be dangerous. All this fucking safe stuff . . . it's insidious as death.'

'Most art is bad,' said Mrs Frampton. 'Very few paintings come off. Hardly ever.'

Her daughter had looked at her and away. She thinks it's my depression speaking, Mrs Frampton had thought, but it's not. Let them get on with their bad paintings. Keeps them out of mischief and you never know. Pigs might fly.

Mireille and her boss, the youngish Monsieur Paul, proved to be unexpectedly useful and co-operative. Theirs was a small agency, and the season was slow. Both were locals, which proved to be invaluable. Monsieur Paul was the son of a builder, a sturdy man with a drinker's nose, but with a good eye and a quiet wit. Mrs Frampton moved from her hotel to a small *pension* between the farm and the town, and Monsieur Paul senior set about alterations necessary for her to be able to take residence within her new acquisition. She bought a Renault, and flew about the country roads. There were setbacks. Delays. The weather, non-arrival of materials, frequent disappearances, in typical fashion, by Monsieur Paul on other projects, were teeth-grinding.

Her friends Noddy and Jeff came from Bradford for ten days, and helped to dig out the stream. She wrote letters, made long reports to Chloe on the telephone, and wrote to Mother Caterina, who replied with brief summaries of progress at the residence, and wishes for her good health.

All summer the workmen chipped and dug, renewed flooring, carving away rot and scarfing-in new wood with a discreet reticence. Mrs Frampton, her head covered against the dust, cleared out the rooms and marvelled at what she found. There were old brass bedsteads, smaller iron beds with scrolling flowers, a wrought iron cot, a washstand needing only new white marble, the back still intact with lucent turquoise tiles. Several of the old chairs in the barn she put together again, a rocker, and two heavy elbow chairs. The sofa in the living-room, with its faded rose-coloured cover and tassels, she hauled to Nice to be remade in the same style and colour. Chloe, on a brief visit with the new baby, George, an amiable, contemplative person who lay in his cot with alert, waiting eyes, had shaken her head, but when the sofa was returned agreed that the cumbersome old piece, now with a soft sensuousness, added warmth and a special style to the room.

'It looks like something from Colette.'

Mrs Frampton, noting the heavy blackberries drooping in the open window behind the sofa, breathed deep.

I'll paint that. No. Too obvious. I've have to cut it with something.

She had done no painting since before . . . before everything happened, but, on leaving Paris, had bought a large thick pad and was now sketching. It was useful as a record for the house. It made you look. It reminded, it forced you to see. And take decisions.

'When do you hope to move in?'

'Lord knows, my dear.'

She moved in during the heavy heat of August, cursing herself for her stupidity.

I shall be away from the sea, I shall swelter up there behind that great lump of outcrop.

But the house, with walls two feet thick, girdled by the stream which ran, to her delight, even in high summer, was cool. The ominous chalk whale-hump which was her view shaded the little valley. The grapes from her vineyard were late, said Yvo, but good, large and sweet. She stood with him, watching the scudding shadows from high cloud move across the vines. At least they got the late-afternoon sun. That would be useful in spring and autumn when the angle of the sun was low.

She had not meant to move until October. However, when the electricity was on and water ran from the taps there seemed no reason to stay on at the *pension*. The plasterers were at work upstairs, the plumber was still excavating in the dairy, the sound of the stonemasons echoed in the stable yard as they chopped stone for her walls. Furnishing had been a challenge. She spent long days in the Renault touring towns and villages, looking for simple pieces of furniture, something less heavy than the majestic lumps of walnut planking that had suited Spain. This house, oddly, demanded a simple elegance, not the rusticity she had first planned.

Perhaps it was the sofa. Or perhaps I'm getting Frenchified. She pulled a face. Much chance of that.

None the less, she bought two fine-lined *bergères* in a local auction and had them covered in pale-grey. She found a simple carved-wood cabinet with a glass front that reflected the light from her windows, pleasing her greatly. She ordered good firm beds from her favourite shop in Tottenham Court Road and had them sent out, selling the brass ends for a good price and keeping the little iron bedsteads, refurbished with new mattresses for the attics. She repainted the wrought iron cot herself and dressed it with old *broderie* bought in a market and carefully rinsed back to chalk-white. She had the dog's teeth cleaned and bought him a handsome collar and acquired two half-grown cats from Madame Angelier, who lived down the valley, and called them Plume and Brume.

She rang Emilio, who sent on her linen and china and bits of silver, her pictures and ornaments. Unpacking them, in the long, wide living-room, her things strewn all over the floor, was painful. She sat up on her heels, face shiny with the effort of bending, and felt a deep misery. Here was her life in Spain. Everything was redolent, everything reminded her of her life, her friends. She missed them! There were letters, and she had called Gudrun several times during the summer. Bleak, after her last call, had been the feeling that life was going on, cheerful and festive, without her. As though she had not been. The residence was thriving. The new Polish matron was marrying a local police inspector but carrying on with her post. She picked up a painting of arum lilies by the pool at Casa John.

I painted that just after Little May's birthday. She was sitting on the terrace writing thank-you letters. We hardly spoke all afternoon, and Fortunato chased a ball.

Even worse, many of her belongings seemed not to fit here at La Bastide. She fidgeted from room to room, arranging and rearranging, abandoning the effort more than once.

I'll sell, and buy new ornaments.

After several days of irritability she made up two tea chests and had the builder take them down to the church for a sale in aid of repairs.

There, that's done it. Now I've got nothing, not even a decent tea-set.

You rogue, she thought. And spent a happy week buying new china and glass, an art deco vase for the landing window and a silly iron doorstop.

Chapter 11

W HEN THE NEW china and earthenware had been delivered and arranged, and the glass put away, and the rest of her things from Spain disposed about the farm, making it home and no longer a building site, Mrs Frampton began to think of May's legacy, of the paintings. Perhaps, now, they could come from the bank. There was a bare wall adjacent to the small landing window, with not too much sunlight for the Boudin, a discreet, reticent spot for the blues and yellows and pearly greys. The tiny Corot she would put in her bedroom, on the further wall, high up, to set off the curve of the lake and hide the gleam of the overpainting. She thought with a pang of the Matisse, the glorious Matisse, with the pink madder and bold violet lines delineating the woman at the window, the sure strokes, the effrontery of line, the pure intellect of the picture soaked in the sensuous. It had been a hard wrench. She had invited the people from the Prado to see the painting and they had been alive and happy, thinking that she was going to make a gift of her legacy. But she had asked a fine sum, towards a foundation for education for poor children, where a child might profit by special help. As she had been helped by winning her scholarship to the local grammar school where she had learned to draw, and to understand Turner, and love Sickert and the English school, as her old teacher had done.

The paintings arrived at the end of September and she put them up herself, the older Danguy brother having made secure fittings on the wall.

'Madame will wish for light fittings to display her pictures?'

'No.'

He had shrugged, slightly offended; he was a family man and

given to improvements. She had murmured that the paintings were worthless but old family things, that the light might be damaging to the surface of the paint and he had nodded wisely with Gallic condescension.

My eye was in, she thought, when the pictures were in their appointed spots. They looked, if anything, more supreme in their new positions than at Casa John's where they had been subdued by illustrious rivals.

They gave Mrs Frampton energy and impulse. She scoured the shops of Nice for old damask tablecloths and napkins, for huckaback teatowels that wiped glasses without smearing, for smooth linen sheets, finer than her own, for the long nights. Sleep, still, was an uncertain friend.

By the beginning of November, with her old friend Noddy back for a return visit to help, she had finished the main shopping for the house. The windows were dressed throughout with simple floor-length muslin curtains edged with a cotton braid in soft yellow. They blurred the light while still revealing the fine long lines of the windows. Upstairs the main guest room was graced with a walnut table, on which she set a little Queen Anne dressing mirror, bought many years since at a country auction in England. She remembered often, as she gazed into the silver-dull glass, Vic's face as she had raised her hand and bought the glass for forty pounds. His fury had been awesome. Forty pounds! For a silly little mirror with a couple of drawers under.

Years later she had pointed out a similar, slightly less handsome glass in a Chester shop and dragged him in to ask the price. The woman had been snooty and unimpressed by the Framptons. She had taken ages in the back room, probably hoping that the undistinguished couple would creep humbly away and stop littering her elegant salon. The glass, she said, was priced at six hundred and seventy-five pounds. It was – yes, said Mrs Frampton, using her heaviest accent to offend, I know. Queen Anne. I've a similar one meself, only smaller and prettier . . . worth a lot more. Yours is on the heavy side, clumsy, know what I mean, love. You'll have to drop, I don't doubt. People are getting fussy nowadays. And she had come out

of the shop giggling like a schoolgirl, amazed at her own cheek
but stirred with old memories of having been snubbed at school
for her country accent, when she had crept about, bewildered
by the rush and race of people after the quiet of the farm and
the village. Not to mention old hatreds of the local gentry, so
civil and well mannered when they met you. And who treated
you worse than they treated their animals, keeping people up
at night, feeding them on wretched food below stairs, talking
to one another over your head as though you didn't exist.

She had helped out at the manor when for two blissful terms
she had been a student at the art college before things went
badly at home. Then all those jobs, for the money.

Funny how I got to nursing.

Her friend Phyl had turned up, fresh and smart in her uniform.
And made Mrs Frampton laugh and ooh and ah with her stories.
On a whim she had applied, and had known from her first week
of training that this would do. The money was dreadful, the
probationer hostel grim. None the less, those had been the best
times, those days on the wards, in casualty, in the theatre, your
feet bursting, your eyes pricking with tiredness. There was only
one way to live, and that was in the moment. The moments then
had meant something.

Her own bedroom she furnished in the French style. A Madame
de Silvestre, recommended by the upholsterer in Nice, had, for
a fairly whacking fee, put her in touch with people who wished
to sell things from their homes. Which they no longer had use
for, as it was put to her. She and Noddy had visited two old
sisters in Cannes and Mrs Frampton bought two Empire chairs
and a *chaise-longue* in faded water-silk. From a young man in
Villefranche who was selling up after losing his mother she
bought a gilded elbow chair, a beautiful old wall mirror, green
park chairs for outside and a marble-topped table. The marble
was cracked right across, but the price was good, the wrought
iron beneath comely and the marble itself old and leonine and
gnarled, the corners rubbed smooth by the years. Of all her
acquisitions this pleased her the most. It was upended in the
stable yard until Michel and Jean-Louis, the stonemasons, had

finished paving the terrace to the west, where she could sit and look down towards the stream, and the thick coppices of willow. The willows fascinated her. They grew on both sides of the lane right down to the main road. They were never still and marched almost up to her walls at one point. At first she had thought to ask Yvo to chop, to thin and prune, but decided to leave everything, at least for a season.

Then we'll see.

She contented herself with buying a decent mower, and Yvo cleared an irregular patch down to the water's edge for her to walk and sit with her friends on the green park seats.

After bland, cheerful Noddy, as vacuous as ever, but with her practical hands, had gone home laden with Provençal gifts for her friends and relations, Mrs Frampton experienced a setback. Things seemed to come a halt. She began to make even longer lists, trying to find more and more and more to do. Everything had not gone swimmingly. Jean-Louis had decamped, so the work on the stone walls was going slowly. There had been a plumbing disaster in the end bedroom. The Chinese cabinet and table bought for the little dining-room were all wrong and would have to be resold.

But the kitchen, with its new simple shelves, Belfast sink with the old swan taps, plate rack lovingly built on site by Marcel, the old chippie, pitch-pine draining boards proudly gleaming, geraniums already going leggy on the sills, was a triumph. She sat at the big old table, a *donnée* from a Danguy outhouse, with her lists and notes, drinking Nescafé and large mugs of tea. There *was* plenty more to do. There was plenty! But, in the night when her eyes gave out and she could read no more, it was impossible to fool herself. She had been inspired. She had done a wonderful job. There was not an antique shop, a *brocante* yard, that she had not inspected. She had made her knees filthy crawling through junk, looking for the right door furniture, a fender worthy of her sitting-room. The house was exactly as she wanted it. Simple, cool and underfurnished, with the scullery at the back of the dairy fitted with a huge new skylight and whitewashed for a studio. A studio!

Who do I think I am?

Despite putting them on her lists, so far she had avoided buying paints. She had her crayons, her heavy pencils, her pen and ink, her small sketch books. Now she could get to work.

She knew she could not. And she knew why she could not. She was not in a state of grace. Painting, like writing and singing, like acting and dancing, was loving. She did not love. She did not love at all. She was far, far from love. Nothing, even during these busy, frantic months of activity, had come close to opening the door even a tiny way towards life. She scanned the pictures of her grandchild, Sam, in America, talked to him on the telephone. She listened with interest to Chloe's reports of George, of his placidity, his rapid progress. Inside, little clicks in her head, like the beads of an abacus slotting across, reassured her that her children and grandchildren were well, were alive and living their lives. But there was no joy in it. Only a grudging, bitter relief.

I shall have to wait. I'll fill up the time with odd jobs, sweat out the winter. Then . . . then?

She knew very well what then. She knew what to take, and what dosage. She even had the spot picked out. Across the vineyard and up the long sloping path was a spinney of young chestnut trees, sparse from the chalk on which they grew and bent slightly by the wind. The ground fell away to a small declivity before rising and falling and rising again to the gaunt slopes of the white cliff that brooded over her house and land.

She had discovered the tiny dell on an early walk. The young chestnuts made an almost complete circle, a gap to the east being filled by rosemary and three gaunt brooms. Everything about the spot was significant, of what she did not know. Whenever she walked up there she felt different. She would sit on the one comfortable rock and feel something happening, something inside her head that filled her with restlessness. She castigated herself for silliness.

I'm a silly old woman. A silly old woman of no further use to the world.

Sometimes, to ward off the devilish threat of self-pity, she would try to console herself with modern notions of self-love. If there is no one to love you, the magazine doctor had said, love yourself. Yes, well, she knew all about that. Often at night she held herself down there, using old loves or fictional characters to fire her imagination until she gasped aloud. She had always done this, throughout her marriage. Memories of Vic as a lover were grim. His needs were swift, silent and sullen.

I was his right – a plate to eat off, a pot to piss in. Well, that at least was over.

As November declined towards December, towards Christmas, she stopped walking up to the circle. Time enough. There was no point in marching towards it. You had to give life a chance. You had to display patience. Show willing.

The weather broke suddenly and dramatically. For three days there were thunderstorms, sending the chickens flying across the yard and the dog under the kitchen table. Brume, who had produced three ginger kittens, began to carry them about the house and then wail, bereft. Mrs Frampton, cursing, retrieved one from the dairy, two from behind the bath. The rain settled to a downpour, day after day. The air seemed spun of milk, unbreathable. The willows sagged on to the road. The road itself became a river. The stream overflowed its banks and flooded the pansy seedlings, reaching almost to the terrace. Mrs Frampton, alarmed, rang for advice from her neighbours but was reassured. The water never rose to the house. It came close, but after four days the heavy downpour modified to a mild and persistent drizzle. Mrs Frampton, well stocked with food in her big chest-freezer, stayed at home, preferring not to drive the flooded roads. She sank into torpor, reading detective novels, eating fruit and drinking tea, going to bed early without washing, and, after reading into the small hours, lying in a stupor until late the next morning.

And still the rain fell. Darkness now came early and she switched channels on her television, trying for decent programmes, and ran her old Garbo videos and her Fred Astaires. Sometimes she fell asleep before the set but, sure as houses, once she ascended the old wide staircase and rolled into bed, sleep vanished.

Lying one morning in bed, looking out at the thick wet

greyness, she thought: I haven't seen a soul for a week. I'm becoming a recluse. Should I go out . . . ring somebody up? Does it matter? Will it change the world? No. Forget it, May. You're dispensable.

Instead, she took a bath and lay for an hour in the tub doing crosswords.

Later, after a cold shower to wake herself up, she went out, walking the bounds after feeding the animals. The rain, for the first time in a week, had stopped, but the day was still grey and more rain threatened from the west.

She thought: Shall I go up to the knoll? Why not? I might as well. I'm done here. I've finished everything. There's nothing more to do except fill in time. Why bother?

A spasm of resentment flashed through her, making her head shudder.

I've done my share. More than my share. I haven't been mean. I've been silly, a coward, I haven't taken enough chances, I've given in. But I haven't been bad, a bad person. I've tried to be good. So much for that. Why not? Why not now?

A crow descended on the edge of the vineyard a few feet before her. Then another.

If a third crow flies down, I'll do it.

The two birds pecked, digging their fearsome, efficient beaks into the softened ground, gorging themselves with worms. She looked up as another bird circled over her head.

Come on . . . come on, you devil.

It flew away towards the chalk face then circled and returned. And settled, between the vines, thirty yards away. And waddled towards her. Mrs Frampton turned decisively and walked back to the house.

Chapter 12

THAT EVENING, MRS FRAMPTON cooked herself a good dinner. She took a large fillet steak from the freezer, prepared carrots and potatoes and a side salad from the late-sewn lettuce in her vegetable patch. She made a trifle, enough for two, and decorated it with glacé cherries and hundreds-and-thousands, in the way her mother had done, and poured a pot of cream to go with it. She put out almond biscuits on her silver tray, and her Worcester cup and saucer, and made a light soup from leeks, with a dash of lemon and cream. Again, she made too much, and shook her head. Well, what did it matter?

At seven she switched on the World Service for company, and settled down at table instead of by the fire, to eat in style. She soon became full, managing only a third of the meat. She tried a few spoonfuls of trifle, ate a small ratafia with her tea. A short story on the radio ended inconclusively. Then there was a Sibelius symphony. She listened to the surging harmonies as the wind got up outside and the sounds in the willows grew wilder. More branches down tomorrow.

What does it matter?

She was awoken by a loud knocking.

What on earth . . .?

She stumbled to her feet, alarmed. The sound of the storm outside muffled the sound of voices, men's voices! What was it? She hurried to the door, falling over her footstool, and dragging the lace tablecloth half from the table.

I must have dozed off.

At the door she shouted, 'Who is it? What do you want?' And jumped back as the knocking was renewed, loud and violent.

She made for the bolt and then thought: Why not? If I'm going to be attacked, so be it. She threw open the door.

There, on the step, stood a huge, monsterish figure. Rain fell on his head, plastering hair round his face. His face! What was wrong with his face?!

In a moment she knew who it was.

'Honoré! Come in!'

He lurched towards her and she took his weight, gesturing to the taxi driver for help. In the living-room she sat him down and went to pay the fare. When she returned she paused at the sitting-room door, breathless. Honoré sat across from her, lit only by the flames of the olive logs. She was aware of his long legs, stretching across the rug, and the hair on his wet face. And his face. The left-hand side, further from the fire, was gaunt. The sleek, smooth cheek had gone. Instead there was boniness, planed lines where there had been curves. The other side was a puckered, contorted shapelessness. As she approached, chatting nervously, she noted that the flames had missed his scalp.

At least he has all his hair.

He tried to rise.

'No, sit there. I'll get you a towel and a drink, you look as though you could do with one. Whisky?'

He nodded and began to apologise for his unheralded appearance.

'I have only your address.'

'Didn't I put the telephone number?'

'You were not connected.'

'Oh, that's right. So they've let you out?'

She refurbished her meal for him and he ate, as he had always eaten, with a respectful, silent concentration – ah, that had not gone. But he was far from well. The dark eyes, the right with its sheered-off look due to the scarring, gazed out sombrely in mute accusation. She jumped up and down to serve him, to make coffee from the freshly ground beans she had bought for her moving-in party with the neighbours. He sipped, then drank.

Well, that was all right, then. Which is more than you are, my dear.

She got out the brandy. This made him comatose almost at once so she left him and went upstairs to the main guest room, putting out fruit and Evian and books by his bed. When she came back to the living-room he was asleep. She struggled upstairs with his suitcase and opened it, laying out his shaving things in the new bathroom between the two guest rooms, hanging up his suits, smoothing the grey fabric, taking out his shirts and putting them in the old chest she had bought in Aix.

At the bottom of the case was a folded leather picture frame. Without thinking, she opened it. The pictures were both of Little May. In the left she was standing on the grass, shading her eyes against the sun. She seemed to be speaking, she was so alive! The picture, in no way professional, caught something real, something of the moment. She was saying that the picture would be awful, that the sun was in her eyes. But her mouth was laughing . . . She was protesting but not protesting. The other photograph was a portrait that Mrs Frampton had never seen. It must have been taken twenty years before. Little May was young, a young, fragile girl with pensive, already careful eyes. A most beautiful girl, with hair loose on her shoulders. Honoré, without a sound, appeared at her elbow. Together they gazed down at the photograph. Then Mrs Frampton sighed. She closed the case and laid it on the bedside table.

'Your bathroom is through there. Goodnight, Honoré. The air is good, you'll sleep well, I promise.'

To her amazement she slept herself, almost as soon as she laid her head on the pillow. The harsh croaking of the crows awoke her. She stood by the window, yawning, watching them take the harvest of the rains, moving with their stiff alderman's walk, seeing one another off, rising at the sound of a tractor echoing on the chalk ridge.

Stupid things. Still, they have their place. They got rid of the rubbish.

Something burst in her head. She sat abruptly on the side of the bed.

What on earth have I been on about? I've been going daft. Mental.

She went quickly to her handkerchief drawer and took out the bottles of paracetamol and barbiturates and flushed them down the lavatory.

And that's the end of that! Now. I wonder what he wants for his breakfast.

That morning, under a warm, weak sun, they sat on Mrs Frampton's unfinished terrace and talked and drank coffee, and talked and drank more coffee until her head began to throb and she brought out the Evian. Honoré, as she knew, had been sent to Switzerland, to be treated at the clinic of Professor Galliani.

'They've made a good job of your face,' she lied.

He looked at her, his good side twisting sardonically.

'I mean it – it's much better than it was.'

But his story made her sick. The surgeons had disagreed. There were power politics at the clinic. In the end he had discharged himself and gone to his sisters. Whose wailings had driven him mad. He did not know what to do, where to go. He had taken a plane to Málaga and returned to Casa John, back to his rooms over the stables. But he had been ill at once. The nuns had nursed him, and, after his health seemed to mend, asked him to drive for them. At the wheel he had panicked, and left the same day without warning, staying in Barcelona, then with an old friend in Marseilles.

'I've been drinking a lot.'

'Let me look at your face.'

She inspected his face, touching the ridged scars with her forefinger.

'You're wrong, you know. They did a lot for you.'

'I am a monster.'

The phrase hung on the air. The wind stirred in the trees outside and a crow made its ugly sound, close, then further off.

She looked at him covertly, in the bright, harsh daylight. Now that he was no longer overweight, Honoré was, she saw, a handsome man. With his bad side turned away from her, sprawled in the basket chair, he looked about forty . . . She had always taken him for ten years older.

'How old are you, Honoré?'

'I am forty-seven.'

'You look younger than you did. It must be the loss of weight.'

They sat in silence. Then she rose to cook the lunch, leaving him with the papers.

As she washed a salad she thought: That face isn't good enough. He's had all that suffering, and he looks dreadful. When he turns to face you, it's frightening, with his eye drooping and his cheek all scrunched together. Whatever have they done? Burns shouldn't look like this. It was impossible to say, of course. If the flesh had been removed to the bone . . .? Just the same . . .

She put lamb chops under the grill and went to her desk to thumb through her telephone book. Yes, she still had Jill Furness's number. Jill Furness (as Mrs Frampton still thought of her), her old colleague, who, with her pale skin and endless legs had extracted a surgeon from the arms of his boss's daughter, given him three sons and assisted him to the Elysian fields of St John's Wood. She waited impatiently for a connection. The reply at the other end, when it came, was disappointing. Lady Morton was out of the country and was not expected back until after Christmas.

That afternoon Mrs Frampton wrote to her old friend. Robert Morton was now emeritus, but he would still have pull. He was a sound old thing, unsnotty for a surgeon and a man who had chopped open royalty. Something might be done. Something is *going* to be done, she thought to herself. The man can't bear to look at himself. He used to be a dandy . . . look at him now – everything he wears is creased! She watched him as he bent over the evening meal. He ate slowly, without speaking. He said thank you, and offered to help with the trays. But he was dead, the man was dead. Or seemingly dead.

The trouble is, my son, you are not dead. So where is all the energy going?

In the kitchen, setting up a drinks tray, her own new-found energy waned. What was this new intrusion? It was like a call from the other side, from a world which no longer existed. From a world, she thought, kicking open the door to the living-room, which was inhabited by Little May. She looked across to Honoré, slumped by the fire, a newspaper on his lap.

You belong back there. I've come here to get away from you.

71

He looked up at her and her bowels turned.

Poor bloody creature.

She set the tray down quietly, not to aggravate his nerves.
'Brandy?'

He neither acquiesced nor refused. He waved a hand. She understood. Even to make the decision was impossibly exhausting. She poured a dram for him and put it by his side.

You've got a lot to answer for, my friend. You stopped me. If it weren't for you, turning up like a ghoul at the door with your bloody face, I'd be out of it. If you'd come a day later . . .

They sat by the fire, watching the olive wood spark and glow. Neither spoke.

After half a hour she said, 'I suppose we might as well go to bed.'

He nodded and rose obediently without speaking. She watched him, tall and angular, the new Honoré, climb the wide staircase, his gait stiff and heavy. She opened her mouth to say, Sleep well. And closed it again. He would. He was taking drugs. But would she?

Chapter 13

FOR TWO DAYS Honoré slept late and sat in the garden, gazing out at the looming chalk face, saying little. He was polite always, attempted to rise when she approached, thanked her for his meals, excused himself at eleven to go to his room. Mrs Frampton drove to town in the Renault and began to shop with a new purpose. She searched for food that would be light, easily digestible, delicious; bought paperbacks and hired videos, looking for comedies, for something to make him smile.

On the third day he took a short walk along the verge towards the Ferme Danguy. She watched him from the landing window, and saw him turn back abruptly as two of the lads from the farm came into view over the rise. When he came in she asked if he would like to accompany her to the harbour for coffee. She knew what the answer would be but was unprepared for the betrayed look on the ruined face.

The poor man. How *could* he go out, looking like that? Mrs Frampton was used to the stares of the ignorant. She had on many occasions acted as escort for the residents of Casa John. People would stare, snigger, blench, draw away. There had been occasions when the little parties were asked to leave premises, vacate a café terrace for fear of upsetting so-called normal patrons. She had learned to swallow her indignation and go. She had also learned to get her own back in devious ways, not to waste her energies, but to punish. A restaurant owner on the road to Estepoña found ordure dumped on the edge of his property. Sorry, said the local authority, we can do nothing for you. A lakeside property owner who had screamed at Mrs Frampton and the nuns to clear off and take their idiots with them was stricken by a sudden and inexplicable tax demand, and a surprising lack of support from the *presidente* of his pueblo. The

Sisters, hearing Mrs Frampton on the telephone to her friends and allies, would shake their heads and purse their mouths. Forgiveness was all. And an eye for an eye, she would respond, winking, making them smile despite themselves.

This was different. The trouble was that Honoré (there was no arguing) was horrific. You had to force yourself to look at him. Out of the tall body, now narrow and high shouldered, his neck stuck out of his clothes. Worse was the comeliness of one side of his face. It made him look like a nightmare from a movie, a *Dorian Gray* spectre. She shopped alone, tempting him with lobster, with fresh *daurade* lightly steamed in a lemon sauce, with small pots of caviare. Some of which he ate, but without lustre, so there was no joy in it for either of them. Mostly he sat, gazing out at the gaunt, grey edifice which crouched like a vast marine animal, green at the bottom, the low trees and shrubs fringing the base like seaweed. There was nothing to do but wait until Jill Furness came back from abroad. She had mentioned the subject to Honoré, gently affirming her opinion that a great deal more could be done for him. His response had been to favour her with a defensive look almost of hate.

Yes, she thought. They've messed you about. They've saved your life and you don't think it's worth it. You don't think you deserve to live. Looking in the glass, you think they must loathe you to make you look so bad. You were a good-looking man. You took it for granted. You had that genial condescension for the plain, the ill made, the undistinguished. Well, it's natural. But now you know what it's like. To be the rest of us. The old, the fat, the unbeautiful.

None the less his presence as her guest gave her occupation. She had a shape to her day now. Soon it would be Christmas. Afterwards, perhaps they could go south. She might hire a house, somewhere secluded, Morocco, perhaps, where he could sit in the sun. The nights were now cold on the farm and she switched on the ancillary heating, noticing that he seemed cold all the time. She would not give up the idea of further treatment. She would bide her time. On the other hand, he might decide to up and go. He had come uninvited: might he not take off in the same way, perhaps without saying goodbye, giving her warning?

I must be prepared for that. The man is not in charge of himself. If I wake up one morning and he's gone I'll do something at once. I'll go to Chloe or take a trip to Michael and Steffi and Sam. I mustn't let the shock do me in. I can't stop him. If he disappears I must not allow myself to worry. It isn't in my power to do more than I am doing.

She put away her fears, tidying them as she tidied her drawers, and kept to rituals, placated by Honoré's presence in the house, and at the same time alarmed by the sickness in him. One night, in the small hours, she heard him making a noise in his room. She got up and listened at his door. Was he snoring? But the sounds were the sounds of weeping. She lifted her hand to knock, and then crept quietly back to bed, and soon the noises ceased.

Two nights later something happened that was very surprising indeed. Together they had watched a video of *Mon Oncle*, supper trays on their laps. Neither of them had laughed aloud, but the atmosphere had been perceptibly lighter, and, making his tisane for the night, she felt almost cheerful. At about two o'clock she was woken by dreadful sounds from his room and rushed straight in. He was lying half out of bed and making strange coughing noises, drawing in his breath and heaving like an animal in travail. Seen by the light from the landing he looked enormous, jerking to and fro as she grasped him and held him to her, murmuring into his hair.

'Now, now . . . that's enough. You're all right, my dear . . . it's all right now . . .'

Within a moment he had rolled on top of her and they were one. She was so surprised that she opened her legs almost in the same movement. The mutual orgasm was instant and he sighed, with a loud groan, and lay still at her side. She lay on her back, eyes and mouth open in shock. She couldn't . . . it wasn't . . . it hadn't happened. It could not have happened. She lay very still, her thighs wet, listening to his regular breathing. He was asleep. She said softly, 'Honoré?' but there was no reply. Very quietly she slipped off the bed and went back to her own room. She lay on her back, shivering slightly from shock, to try and think about what had happened. She dozed, and woke, then fell into a deep sleep. She was wakened by the cheerful whistle of the stonemason under her window.

However long have I been sleeping?

She took a quick shower and went down to make breakfast. It was ten o'clock! Was he up? She made the coffee and boiled two eggs. Should she take in a tray? What should she say to him? Should she ignore it? He was on barbiturates . . . he might not even remember . . .

If he says nothing, I'll say nothing.

As she crossed to the boiling kettle there was a sound behind her. He was at the kitchen door, standing in the way she was now so accustomed to, with the right-hand side of his face turned away from her.

'Thank you so much.'

He approached, and in his hands were flowers, two late roses and some rosemary twigs.

'Oh, where did you find them?'

'Beyond the stream. You can see the remains of flowerbeds.'

'I know. Later on I'm going to make a winter garden there. It's sheltered. We'd better eat here, I think, it looks miserable outside.'

They ate their breakfast in easy camaraderie. Once or twice she darted a glance at him, and the third time he caught her at it and smiled his dreadful, twisted smile. He put out his large hand.

'We are friends, are we not?'

She held his hand between her own for a long moment and looked at him, right at him, at the terrible face.

'Yes. We are.'

She got up to make him more toast.

Chapter 14

N O TWO DAYS were the same. As his strength returned, Honoré threw himself into the improvements at the farm, bullying Michel, who was terrified of him, and drinking with Léo and Albert, the two gypsies who came to help with the walling. And who teased him, seeming quite unperturbed by his face.

'What happened to you, amigo . . . did she set the dog on you?'

'So the husband found out, hah . . . caught in the act, eh?'

Their gibes were silly and uninventive. But they were healing. Honoré was a man among men. In the old days, when Casa John had been Casa Morisca and Little May was a reclusive widow, Honoré, an assiduous protector and confidant, had none the less led a life of his own. He had been a fanatical football fan, he had ridden horses, fished and hunted. Now he bent over the rocks, building her winter garden, making paths so that she did not get her feet covered with mud. He cleaned out the rooms over the stables and treated the ironwork and painted it shining black. Once or twice he came into town with her. Always, he stayed in the car. They would pore over lists and she would come back to the car once, twice, three times, for advice, to show him nails, a brand of paint. He began to listen to the news and they took the dog for walks. Then he mended Madame Angelier's fence, knocked down by the storms and rain. She, short-sighted, had said to him one day, 'What have you done to your face? Oh, well, it will heal.' And gave him some herbs to steep for it, which he showed to May with his one-sided smile.

Their life during the day was one of easy friendship. Upstairs was different. He moved into her room. They changed her small double bed for the two singles in the guest room, locking them together. Every night she went up first. Every night he joined her. Sometimes they lay awake together talking quietly of trees, of journeys he had made in earlier days, when he had been a diplomatic courier. Sometimes she told him of her home, of the farm on the Welsh borders, of her old dog Tip, of winning prizes at school. They talked of France, of early climbing holidays with his sisters, of days in Normandy, of his uncle, Alphonse, who had taken him to the placid local brothel as a sixteenth-birthday present, to inaugurate him into the world of sex.

'But I had already loved my schoolfriend, Emilienne.'

'Did you tell him?'

'No, no, it would not have been polite.'

Sometimes they lay without speaking. Once or twice she took up the cassette player and they listened to music until she heard his regular breathing.

Other nights were different. She always knew when it was coming. He would look at her, his twisted face worse than usual, almost accusing. On those nights she felt a black smiling within. It wasn't that she felt wicked, that she was doing wrong, was off in some way. It was a sort of inner triumph. Something was winning. Something inside her jeered and laughed. A different May was emerging, for the first time in her life. A May that she was unacquainted with, a May she did not understand at all. She had always thought of herself as someone with a not very successful body, a body that was too sturdy, not elegant. A body made for work, not for pleasure. A body that was mundane, not sensual. Now this was changing.

He was infinitely delicate. At first their conjoining was silent, needful and mutually swift. That soon changed. He began to murmur and play with her, touching her in a way that at first she found alarming. When she automatically moved away he soothed her. He made her laugh, and, one night, switched the light on, embarrassing her horribly. She sat up on the edge of the bed and struggled to put on her nightgown. But he pulled her round to face him, and explored her body. The glimpse of his face made her submit . . . what could she do? If this was what he wanted . . . But he sensed her reaction and shook her gently. So she looked at him and said she knew she was an ugly old woman. He had gone on perusing her, his head back on the pillow.

'You have high breasts for a woman with two children.'

'Hard work, I expect.'

'I noticed them. In Spain.'

'Did you?'

Feeling a new daring, she stood up and walked across the room, aware of his gaze behind her. This was something she had never done – with Vic it had always been in the dark. She turned and grinned at him.

'You don't look old, you are like a kid.'

She threw her dressing gown at him, enveloping his head.

Their games became absorbing. Sometimes he went too far, but usually he seemed to know exactly the moment that she was unwilling. Never once did he insist, though sometimes, from a wilfulness that she did not know that she possessed, she messed him about. They both began to sleep better. After struggling with the land outside, heaving furniture in the attics, they would fall asleep, separately or together, and the sex would happen the next morning. Once all morning. Only once did he become so strong, so violent, that the weight and the force of his body made her feel ill after. Later that day she realised that it was Little May's birthday. Did he know? She did not ask.

He began to prowl among her things and criticise her clothes.

'This colour is not good, it does not help your skin.'

Out went the useful grey dress.

'There is a place in Nice. I will take you.'

That had been a *fête* day. Did he mean that he would come into the shop with her? Show himself? The shop had been on a side street, its window displaying two pieces of exquisite lingerie. They went in together and, his face averted from the woman who served them, he chose a *peignoir* trimmed with heavy old lace. She tried it on, and felt like Marie Antoinette. She was measured for brassières, Honoré lounging at the door of the fitting room with no one in the least disturbed. She bought three nightdresses, not even asking the price. Honoré had paid the bill despite her protestations. She knew that he could afford to pay. His father had left him comfortably situated and Little May's legacy had been princely.

They ate out together for the first time on that day, choosing a discreet fish restaurant. There, the happiest moment of the delicious, extravagant outing occurred. The proprietor, looming up behind them unobserved, his approach muffled by street traffic, had glanced at Honoré full-on before he had had time to avert his face.

'Ah, blessé, eh?'

And he had nodded, and asked what they wanted, without blenching or darting horrified looks. She had felt Honoré's soul expand.

Later, she asked him to stop the car, and ran into a shop to buy him socks, silk ties and a cigar cutter. These he had accepted with a Frenchman's avidity, poring in his room over the ties and pronouncing them satisfactory. He was such a mixture of brusque masculinity and piddling French fussiness.

He taught her how to dress a salad, using walnut oil and basil. They began to cook together and he told her that her early meals had daunted him.

'You never said. I thought it was because you weren't feeling well.'

'Only in part.'

'No wonder the dog got fat.' (He had confessed to sliding his food out of the window.) 'Didn't you like the roast beef?'

'It was too cooked.'

One morning she watched him as he joked with the plumbers who had come to dig out a cracked pipe. The sound of his deep laugh stopped her on the stairs as she ascended with clean sheets. The boys from the farm, Yvo and Marc, their father, Monsieur Henri, yes . . . Michel, Léo and Albert the gypsies . . . they all knew him now. But the plumbers were strangers, and he was standing at the gate and talking and laughing with them as though . . . as though his face was not destroyed.

I expect the word has gone about. They'll have been forewarned.

At lunchtime he was nowhere to be found. Since they ate lightly in the middle of the day, she put aside the eggs for the omelette, and, when he returned, nearer four than three, he was drunk. He had been down to the bar in the tiny village, joined the regulars at the poker table in the back room.

That night he was playful and inventive, tender and gentle as always, but demanding, deep into the night.

'You're too much for me.'

'No, I am kind.'

'I know. Just the same.'

The next morning, at the breakfast table on the newly finished verandah with its glass roof, she put down her bowl of coffee.

'Honoré . . .?'

He looked up from his paper.

'I . . .'

'What is it?'

She shook her head at the kindness in his tone and twisted the napkin on her lap.

'Nothing. It's just . . . what do you want from me? It can't be right. I'm an old woman.'

'Don't you like me?'

The good side of his face was towards her, and his expression was mocking.

'Of course I like you.'

He leaned over and put his arms on the table.

'Don't you like what I do with you?'

She felt the blush creep down her neck and chest. It was all very well, but this was daytime.

'Don't you?'

'Oh, stop it.'

'Then why do you ask?'

'I don't know what we're doing, that's all. You're young enough to be my son.'

'I am not your son.'

'What are you, then?'

She felt a sudden, desperate need for affirmation, for something reassuring, of substance. He leaned over the table again, picking up a piece of fresh bread that she had brought up that morning from the village square.

'I am your friend. We are friends.'

81

'I know we're friends. We were friends before.'

There was a small silence. He crumbled the bread thoughtfully, thinking his French, logical thoughts.

'We are loving friends.'

There was another silence and then he spoke again, seeming to sense her need for more.

'You have helped me. I was not in a good way.'

'You mean you're grateful?'

'Of course. As you are to me.' That made her look up. 'You, too, look different now. Absolutely.'

It was true. He had become even franker over the shortcomings of her wardrobe and had thrown out clothes *en masse* one morning with Mrs Frampton squeaking protestation behind him. There had been repeated journeys to Nice, not only to the dressmaker but to the hair stylist. Under his watchful eye Mrs Frampton's hair was cut into a short, stylish shape which gave her a neck and made her look many years younger. Colour was discussed at length, so that now her hair was a deep red with lighter streaks. This latter transformation had been so overwhelming that she had burst into tears in the salon, causing crisis, with Monsieur Gilles wrongly assuming her disappointment. She had had to sniff that she was crying with joy, and send him gold cuff-links as a thank-you gift to calm his feelings.

At the breakfast table she sat in silence, digesting Honoré's words. He was saying that they were friends. Loving friends. That they were grateful to each other.

'What you're saying is we have a good effect on each other.'

'Yes.'

Without looking up from his paper he nudged his bowl for more coffee.

'I see. In that case . . .'

She paused, making him raise his eyes.

'Come to bed.'

His face, in the full view of the February sun, was more hideous than usual, making her blench involuntarily. Which he saw. He rose and reached over the table, taking her by the arm so that the coffee pot went flying and liquid dripped over the white cloth and on to the floor. Without speaking a word he manhandled her up the stairs.

Chapter 15

FROM THEN ON, Mrs Frampton drowned. She went beneath the waves of herself into a physicality that all her life had been denied her. There were days when she was virginal. He courted her. Nights when she became, to her own wonder, coarse and inventive, she who after years of working in hospitals knew bodies well, knew how to touch for comfort, but never till now to incite. He bought a book and they looked at it. She giggled and threw it at him. But that night she was the leader. Once she picked up a belt and hit him, the buckle catching him on the side of his face. It looked like a accident and he took it as such, reeling, his eyes watering with pain. But it was not an accident. She was going down deep into areas of herself. She was finding her own cruelty. She was not a good person any more. But not bad, either. She was someone different. Someone new. On the edge of old age, she came into her privilege, her rights.

She trimmed his hair and massaged him, and cut his toenails. She washed and ironed and pressed his clothes every time he went out, brushing his wide-brimmed hat. She read to him when his mood was restless, was silent when he was remote. She pored over French cookery books and Madame Angelier came stooping up the back path to advise on local dishes. The old woman scurried about in the kitchen, glad to have a mission, once bringing her granddaughter, a whey-faced woman called Louise, who had been abandoned by her spouse and who shelled peas listlessly by the window. She was, however, a dab-hand at making bread and showed Mrs Frampton the French way, and how to make croissants and brioches.

The garden began to burgeon. Mrs Frampton had planted very little, but wild narcissi bloomed in the vineyards and along the edges of the paths. It was time to plant vegetables and start off seeds in trays. Early one morning, as she was bending over a box of seedlings, the telephone rang. Honoré took the call.

'May . . . it is for you!'

She went in, wiping her hands on her sacking apron.

'May? Am I speaking to May Frampton?'

The voice at the other end was precise and authoritative.

'Jill!'

'It's you. I'm sorry not to have replied to your letter – Robert and I were in Italy, then the Seychelles, and we've been in Andermatt for three weeks.'

'Skiing?'

'Robert still skis, I don't, but we've been with friends of my daughter.'

The conversation went along without hurry.

'Whereabouts on the Côte d'Azur?'

Mrs Frampton clarified her whereabouts.

'Oh, down that way.'

The Mortons, it appeared, owned a villa near Vence. Where, said Jill Furness, the weather was entirely more reliable.

Mrs Frampton agreed humbly and thought to herself: My God, she's got very grand. Furness had always had an eye to the main chance, not to mention the marvellous legs and a lot of fair hair she was always messing about with. I wouldn't have fancied her myself, mouth too mean, and she had nasty habits – Sister Furness had been famous for noisy eating and picking her nose. She was one of those subjective people who seemed unconscious of the awareness of others. There were people like that. They often did well for themselves, indeed it was better to let them since they became a damned nuisance when they didn't get their own way. Fortunately, their ambitions were usually mundane and restricted by lack of imagination . . . though occasionally in history you got an Adolf Hitler. Lady Morton talked and Mrs Frampton listened. The upshot of which was an invitation to visit Les Mimosas, where the retired surgeon and his spouse would be in residence come the end of the week. After the call, Mrs Frampton slyly asked Honoré if he would do her the favour of driving her to Vence in ten days.

'I don't want to drive myself.'

'Pourquoi?'

She said she had been feeling headachy. That she hated driving.

'No, you don't.'

She described the Mortons.

Honoré, after her mimicry, agreed to act as her companion for the weekend.

'I dare say they'll find you a bed.'

'If you wish I dress as chauffeur. It's more simple.'

'Not as simple as you.'

In the event, it was another three weeks before they took to the road. Lady Morton, it appeared, had domestic troubles. She was on the telephone a good deal which Mrs Frampton, enjoying the female company, did not mind at all. They talked over old friends and colleagues, and laughed over the ways of the French and foreigners in general. Mrs Frampton referred only briefly to her previous life in Spain, and Lady Morton, after a first reassured cluck when she learned that Mrs Frampton's address had been Marbella rather than Benidorm, was fortunately not of an enquiring mind. She preferred to relate her own experiences, give advice and information, rather than the reverse. Beyond asking if Mrs Frampton knew Prince Alfonso (Mrs Frampton lied and said yes), she made no query as to the reason for her change of address.

She lives in France so France is the best, thought Mrs Frampton. It wouldn't occur to her to ask, thank God.

Two days before they left for Vence, with Honoré safely down at Madame Angelier's clearing gutters, Mrs Frampton rang Lady Morton and explained that her dear friend Honoré Duvalier was staying with her after a serious car accident. She herself was worried that, despite the best treatment that Spain and Switzerland could afford, her old friend was still severely scarred. She said she felt bound to warn her hosts of his appearance, since he had kindly consented to drive her to Vence. Would Jill mind if he were to be included in her kind invitation? Jill would not. And of course, added Mrs Frampton gratefully, unlike the public at large, they would not be distressed by the sight of his disfigurement. She felt the interest rise at the other end and Jill Furness began to ask pertinent questions, revealing the best of herself. Who had treated him in Switzerland? She took down the names of the hospitals, the clinics, and the surgeons.

'I'll ask Robert.'

'You are good. He was always the best.'

Mrs Frampton was so pleased with the conversation that she decided to give her old colleague the peach tree on the small rootstock that she had just planted in a handsome Chinese pot.

The journey to Vence was uneventful. Honoré, quick on the uptake, wore a beautifully cut grey suit and a pale cashmere scarf. Mrs Frampton, her hair newly washed and trimmed, and wearing a silk suit in deep apricot, chosen by Honoré from the Yves St Laurent shop in Nice, began to have kittens as they left the farm. They went out so little. They had each other. There were neighbours, support was mutual and there if you needed it, but otherwise you were left to your own blessed privacy. It was the old country way. Your door was open, but treated with discretion by those around you. She sighed with pleasure. How quickly she had settled back to the ways of her early youth. Then she smiled to herself. The ways of her youth? This *was* her youth. She was living it now, every day, savouring and enjoying every moment.

I am Jane Eyre, she thought. I have my Mr Rochester – I have my reward! Whether I deserve a reward is another matter. But we suffered bereavement. And now we're getting better.

The right side of his face was towards her. She breathed in, smelling his faint, lovely smell and the slight smell of the Hungary water that she had bought for him. He was wearing leather gloves and she watched his hands on the wheel.

I love his hands as much as anything. His hands and his knuckles, and his long sinewy forearms. And the long shanks of his legs. And his flat shoulders.

The nerves engendered by the forthcoming visit began to fall away. She slipped into a stupor and hardly had the energy to swivel her legs to get out as Honoré pulled up outside a bar on the edge of Vence.

They had an aperitif and drove on. Les Mimosas turned out to be a villa in the old Riviera style, Italianate with a gazebo, standing in its own grounds.

This lot wants cutting back, thought Mrs Frampton, as they snaked their way up the drive. The over-mature trees and shrubs gave the property a dated, elderly appearance. Funny how people regarded growth as immutable. It never occurred to so many of them to take down a hideous tree, a fir gone gaunt at the base, a huge shrub taking light from a window. At the front of the house, with its bright-blue doors and window frames which gave it a surprised look, was a vast area of ginger gravel.

Jill Furness was on the steps to greet them. She was wearing a speckled sheath dress that was too young for her, and spiky shoes. Her teeth had gone back and she had had a facelift, but the legs, thinner than ever, looked even better than in the old days. Her face, when she saw Mrs Frampton, was bewildered.

She doesn't recognise me!

The last time they had met was at a charity dinner, several years before Mrs Frampton and her husband had left England.

I was three stone heavier and had a tight perm, she thought, as Lady Morton kissed her three times on the cheek in the 'in' way.

Honoré was introduced and Lady Morton's glance was for a moment professional. Then she did something lovely. She took his face in her hand and turned it so that the light was on the scarred wreck of his cheek.

'Mmm, that's interesting. Do you mind if I have a look? I used to do this sort of thing. You need some more work here. You must talk to my husband. He can give you a much better face than that.'

That was old Jill. Straight in, looking the patient in the eye and demanding courage and co-operation.

Honoré, taken aback, could say nothing. He looked for a split second at Mrs Frampton, and the look signalled betrayal.

'Honestly, Jill, you'll put Monsieur Duvalier to flight. Forgive her, Honoré, once a professional . . . Honoré's had more than enough of hospitals for the time being, alas.'

'Is that so?' asked Jill Furness, taking his arm and walking on ahead, leaving Mrs Frampton with a tiny pang of murderousness.

She heard him say that it had not been easy, and Jill Furness, still arm-in-arm, agreed, and then they were through to the garden and Robert Morton appeared from a path below the serried roses to greet them. He had always been an impressive man, with his silvery grey hair and penetrating eyes. His voice, soft, deep and reassuring, made you feel, well – well, loved, wanted, and able to do whatever he asked of you. To please him. Mrs Frampton, following the others to the terrace for lunch, was reminded of the old days, of this clever man's achievements, of his way with child patients, with those in pain.

He's just the same as he always was. He's like the cowman . . .

You could always tell the cowman on a farm, he was the man with the soft, slow voice, the silent tread. Anything put cows off their milk, a strange face, a wisp of flying paper, an unfamiliar voice. It wasn't that Robert Morton, now Sir Robert, wasn't social. The modulated tones murmured the right noises, but for some reason it didn't put you off as it so often did when men, in particular, played those hateful class games. It was as if he had taken notice of the rules and played the game as and when necessary in order to get where he wanted. They were alike, he and his wife, in their social ruthlessness. They dropped people, and had given offence and hurt, Mrs Frampton knew, on their road to the London consultancy, and to profitable private practice. At the same time they played by the rules. They were patrons of the arts. They gave generously, if to fashionable charities. They took care of poor relations and undertook boring civic duties.

It was just, she thought, looking at them obliquely over the table, it's just that you lot never seek to question the bloody rules, let alone change them. For the better. In the end, never mind all the good you do, you're on the make. It's Jack first.

She sighed over the modest offering on her plate and, at

Robert Morton's quizzical eyebrow, laughed and made a joke about being unable to resist such a delicious pudding. And avoided Honoré's glance.

'You're thinner than you were,' said Jill Furness in an accusing tone as they sat in the garden after dinner that night.

She began to ask questions with a direct and graceless curiosity. Mrs Frampton told her that Honoré was an old business associate of her dear friend, Madame Liu, who had died in a car accident. She managed this without her voice changing. But with difficulty. Jill Furness, who read the social columns, became animated. By the end of their conversation she had the impression that Honoré was a not unimportant tycoon – well, no harm if it kept them happy, though it was likely to affect the bills. Why not give them what they wanted, so long as they did her bidding.

The next day, on the way home after lunch with the Mortons at their exclusive and repellent club, Honoré was silent.

He knows. He knows that this was a put-up job. And that it is my doing.

She said nothing, waiting for his lead, but he put on one of her favourite cassettes of Chopin studies and they sat in the car for several minutes after they drew up in the stable yard, to hear the last harmonies. Carrying her bag he followed her into the house. There was nothing for it but to turn and face him.

'Well, Honoré?'

He shrugged with his slow, inimitable French shrug, and pulled his mouth down, twisting the bad side of his face, making it look even worse.

'Don't do that.'

She leaned up, and kissed his cheek.

'If anyone can make you look better, Bob Morton can. East Grinstead is the best in the world. They learned their job on the airmen during the war.'

He flinched and muttered, 'Yes. This is what he told me.'

She felt him tremble slightly. He stood, head down, immobile. She took his arm.

'It will be worth it. I promise. You have the courage for it.'

'You can say.'

'I know, I know.'

They walked down to Madame Angelier's where the old woman was shredding celeriac and the pallid Louise sat on the back porch drying her long fair hair. Madame brought out the Armagnac and Mrs Frampton regaled her with gentle gossip about their visit to Vence, the old woman nodding and clacking her false teeth. She had been a gadabout in her youth and loved to hear what was going on. She enquired about the ensembles, and, more particularly, about the menus served, and smiled with satisfaction as both Honoré and Mrs Frampton described the fare at the *maison* Morton. She sucked her teeth and nodded briskly, her manner implying that it was no wonder that they had fared badly since their hosts were English. Would Madame Frampton and Monsieur Duvalier perhaps care to break a crust at the *domaine* Angelier? They were most welcome.

It was a way out of the evening for both of them, and, after a delicately flavoured supper, they sat with the Angeliers and watched a video of *Marie Walewska*. And agreed with Louise that Charles Boyer was more than a match for the incomparable Garbo, a worthy *parti*.

On the way back to the farm Honoré stopped. The thin, pale moon was over the chalk ridge. He stood and looked at it, jingling the change in his pocket. Then he turned to Mrs Frampton, his face inhuman in the moonlight.

'D'accord,' he said.

Chapter 16

THE SUMMER SEEMED to fly away so quickly that she could hardly remember one detail, a single event. First there was the journey to London, then the familiar return to hospital routine, to visiting hours, to shopping for the patient. Honoré stayed in London at first for assessment to be made. Consultations led to consultations, colleagues were invoked.

During this time Mrs Frampton, adroitly avoiding an invitation by Jill Furness to stay at her house in St John's Wood, none the less spent a good deal of time with her old colleague, whose life was busy, but who seemed short of real pals. They shopped together and went to the cinema in the afternoons, and took tea at the Ritz. Jill Furness showed off, but the feeling of gratified good will was mutual.

We've both made it, I suppose that's it, thought Mrs Frampton, following Lady Morton's big arse along the broad marble aisles of Harrod's perfumerie.

She took a quick few days in Devon, and played with the children and gossiped with Patrick, who had been in China. And held the baby, Georgie, feeling the pull like electricity in her arms. Oh, how dreadful it was for those who never experienced this, who, by mistake or foolishness or tragedy denied or were denied their birthright. This was the centre of it. Here was the beginning of someone new, someone to take it on, learn, feel, think and give something to this elegant, poignant planet, this planet under siege, this kidnapped woman of a planet, ravaged by Goths.

You'll be there, George. You'll go on.

How could you learn to share, except through your young, those you adored so much that you would give your life for them? Where else were you to learn patience, trust, how to stay tender

91

at the core? God knows, it was hard to understand how a world so evil could have survived, emerged into any sort of decency at all. Most people, more than ever, seemed only after what they could get and devil take the hindmost. But when you had children you had to care. They were your underbelly. They kept a gentleness in your soul, however tough a tycoon you might be. If that went you were done for.

Earlier, doing private nursing in the years when Vic was building up the business, she had met some of those sad old swine, those rich, lonely men who had chosen to be beasts, those frozen, powerful women who held family purse strings, kept their children as supplicant serfs. They made bad deaths. It wasn't worth it, all the money, the power, the houses, the titles, influence. Come your late sixties, however strong, however vigorous, however fertile you'd been, the memory began to go, the sinews betrayed you. It was shocking, a shock. That which you'd always trusted, taken for granted, became not only unreliable but an enemy. Or a whining dependent. Help me! Too late, too late.

Back in East Grinstead she visited Honoré daily. His face went through changes.

'Ooh, you look nice this morning, you look like a pork chop, have a sprig of parsley.'

He never responded to her English humour, but he would, if he could, manage a rictus of a smile for politeness. He was in pain. Sometimes his dark eyes were full of hate and accusation, shouting till the nurse came with another injection. But his face was improving. The lower cheek was no longer contracted. Now they began to work around his eye. He lay in darkness and she read to him, mostly thrillers and adventure stories, sometimes the news from the French papers, stumbling over the sports pages in her awkward French. Chloe came and visited the bedside, and turned to her mother, appalled, in the corridor.

'My God! He looks dreadful!'

'That's the swelling. It'll all go down.'

'His face looks like nothing on earth, Mum. Are you sure it's going to be worth it . . . poor man!'

Her eyes on her mother were accusing.

Mrs Frampton was sharp in reply, calling her daughter a fool, and Chloe, sensing her mother's anxiety, shut up. They shopped for the baby together and gossiped, and Chloe went home. And Mrs Frampton visited, and waited, and talked to the doctors.

The swelling began to subside.

At the beginning of September she returned to the farm to prepare for Honoré's journey home. It was a joyous homecoming. She was greeted by Marc and Yvo and Monsieur Henri himself, and by Madame Angelier, who had made a fish terrine in her honour. Even Louise, now that her divorce was finalised, looked less drab, and came to the back door with a plaited loaf and a basket of lemon cakes and brioches. Mrs Frampton gave them her small gifts and glasses of Armagnac that they seemed to swill like tap water and which sent her to sleep in five minutes. She tried to stay awake as they told her the news. The chalk lorries, which quarried on the south side of the ridge, were a worse nuisance than ever, Monsieur Henri was suing over the destruction of his road. A fox had taken seven of Mrs Frampton's chickens but not Yvonne, her favourite speckly. Patrice, the dog, had had bad ticks and Edouard, from the village bar, had burned them off with his cigar. Marc's wife, Juliette, had had twins.

'I said it was twins!' cried Mrs Frampton, and they toasted her wisdom and showed her a picture of the two little boys, heads lolling in their imperial christening gear.

There was a good deal to be done on the farm. Mrs Frampton, in the months of sitting about, had made plans and set them in motion from a distance. By the side of the dairy the large hole for a swimming pool was already excavated. Taking the idea from Casa John, she had the pool half inside the old outhouse, its stonework newly repointed, and half in the open. The style was simple, and she would plant stone pines for shade, and shrubs against an occasional east wind. Inside, the old barn would be a small gymnasium for Honoré. With a bar and refrigerator. She had been worried that the alterations would spoil the timeless look of the farm, but, tucked in as it was and with the dark-green tiling, much queried by the contractor, the pool would look, with its irregular shape, as natural as it was possible.

There was more work to be finished inside the house. The room next to Honoré's was to be fitted with wardrobes made in the old style, of old wood, for his clothes. He needed proper places for his suits, his shirts, his hats, his shoes. Now he could dress in decent privacy, with mirrors in the right places. He would have a gentleman's dressing room, in the old way.

She got after the builders with a vengeance, bearding them in their own homes as they sat over their *daubes*, in bars as they discussed foxy arrangements with developers. It must, it must all be finished before her invalid friend arrived home! Could they not understand, this was a man who had suffered! She let it be known that Honoré had received his terrible scars in the attempt to save a life, and extorted solemn promises that he should never be made aware that this was known. Here was a modest hero, a gallant man. Was he to be failed by the default of others?

The challenges, thrown down, were picked up. On a clear sunny day in October she drove to Nice airport. Honoré had spent a week in Normandy with his sisters, one of whom would accompany him on the last leg of his journey. But when he came across the concourse to greet her he was alone. She gazed at him. At his face. He gazed back at her. People knocked into them, swirled round and past them. And still she looked up at him, licking away the tears that rolled down her cheeks.

'They did it . . .'

She reached up with her gloved hand and touched his cheek. And stepped back, turning him slightly for a better light. The left side of his face was no longer puckered, screwed up into grotesque, twisted whorls of flesh. There was still scarring. His face looked patched, and slightly bloated. He looked like a boxer who had just been in a prize fight. A handsome boxer. A good-looking man. For the major triumph of the surgeons had been in the work around the right eye. She stood on tiptoe, close, blinking to see better.

'How did they do it!'

He patted his left buttock and laughed, making her heart turn over. His smile – oh, it was a proper smile, not a misshapen gargoyle leer!

'Skin graft.'

They both laughed aloud, she screeching so loudly that people's heads turned and a flock of gulls rose in alarm. She steered him towards the car in the sunlight. He wasn't wearing a hat! His face was open, for everybody to see!

'Is it all right . . . the sunlight?'

'No. Quick.'

On the way home they sang. They sang French ditties, 'Auprès de ma Blonde'; they sang 'Milord', they sang 'My Way' and 'No Regrets'. At the house the neighbours waited with welcoming flowers and cheers and the party went on into the night, though by then Honoré, under doctor's orders, was asleep upstairs, his case unpacked in the new dressing room. Mrs Frampton, very drunk, was assisted to her room at five a.m., having demanded to watch the dawn, but having fallen asleep half-way through her clarion call for companions to join her in a trek to the vantage point on Monsieur Danguy's land. They took off her shoes and tucked her into bed and Patrice the dog, profiting by her insensibility, hopped up and settled peaceably at her feet where he felt he rightfully belonged.

Chapter 17

'I T'S TIME,' SAID Mrs Frampton, lounging in her silk *peignoir* on the verandah, 'for you to think of the future. I mean a career . . . something to do.'

They had talked about this before. Honoré was not a lazy man. In the old days, when he had been chauffeur and bodyguard escort to Little May, he had had a number of irons in the fire, as well as his passionate pursuit of sport. At that time he had been a sleek fifteen-stoner, but strong and never fatigued. You saw him all over the place, musing with an Arab Prince about a horse, at the sailing club, wet and alive after a race, at the bar of the golf club, talking deals with the old men. Now, since his last sequence of operations and the remaking of his face and hand, he seemed content to take each day gently.

At first this pleased Mrs Frampton. They would take a leisurely breakfast under the glassed-in verandah which she had furnished with several small tables and an espresso machine so that it had the atmosphere of a café. (This she had done earlier, in the days when she believed his looks would make him a permanent recluse.) Before breakfast he would plunge into the pool and use the exercise machines. Sometimes she watched him from the water. After breakfast they occasionally took a walk with the dog, but usually he had work in hand. There was plenty to do. Late morning found him at the bar in the village, or at Madame Angelier's, where he was helping with a few modest improvements . . . Mrs Frampton's ambitious endeavours at La Bastide had stirred local energies. It was splendid. As convalescence. As recuperation. But Honoré was a man in the centre of his life. Surely he would want more. Rather than have him lurch into some notion picked up from random conversation, a newspaper article, would it not be more prudent to talk, to plan carefully?

The thought that any plans might well involve his leaving the farm, might take him away from her, did not escape Mrs Frampton. One day, surely, she would lose him. She would have to let him go. Her work was almost done. The post-operative puffiness on his face had subsided. Now he looked like a man with a scarred face. An interesting face. A man who had been in an accident, a war. The marks were there, the lines of incision would remain. But the balance of the face had been restored, its contours almost intact, thanks to Robert Morton and his colleagues. The work had been loving, skilful and successful. The lesions on his hand had been attended to and he had almost full use of it. In gratitude Mrs Frampton sent a massive donation, and was threatened with a visit from Lady Morton. Who fortunately decided that a visit to Romania was the 'in' thing that year.

In himself, Honoré seemed at peace. He was courteous, attentive and thoughtful. True, he had not been to her room since his return from hospital. There were nights when she lay awake, listening for the creak of the door. Would it happen? Was that to be over between them? At first she put it down to his need for recovery. Then she wondered. He was as gentle with her as ever. He rinsed her hair, his interest in her clothes was as sharp-eyed as before, he massaged her neck when she had been reading too long, reminded her of the dentist, her appointment with the *visagiste*. But there was a difference. The increase in kindness, however slight, was a barrier. Mrs Frampton, alone in her bedroom, decided not to worry. The scars might be fading, but the horrific year, the pain that he had undergone, yet again, that was not to be dismissed so quickly. She herself had induced that pain. There were nights, in his agony, when he had cursed at her, begged her, blamed her. And people didn't realise. It took at least two years for the body to recover from intervention. People thought they were well when physical scars had healed. It was not so. Honoré had a journey to make back to wholeness. She must wait. She must take what was offered, with gratitude. And give the thought of resentment a kick out of the door.

One morning, down in the village, a pang of fear invaded. She was in the *boulangerie*, and Madame Spey, handing over her loaves, made a laughing reference to Honoré, and some joke about his desirability as a husband.

'Is it spoken of?' Mrs Frampton had asked casually.

'There are several who would welcome the arrangement. Monsieur Duvalier is well placed, one hears.'

That made her think. Still, it was unlikely that Honoré, spoilt son of a comfortable bourgeois family, would fall for a local girl. There was Madame Rochfort, Aline, the divorcée who lived in the new villa with the pink shutters over the rise. She was well off, and a Parisian. But not as young as she made out. There were the two Valbert girls, both pretty, who worked at the Centre of Agriculture in the nearby market town. All the men looked at them. They lived locally and were the belles of the Café du Monde. But they, surely, were too young. The most likely contender was the Swedish woman, Sigrid, the painter, down the valley. A casual, bony woman, she had style, and once or twice Mrs Frampton had seen Honoré loping off down the path with the dog. Perhaps that was it. Perhaps he was sleeping with her.

Am I jealous? I don't want to think about it.

But then the Swedish woman was suddenly gone and the house and studio sold to a retired pharmacist. And Honoré still took the dog that way for a walk. So that was all right.

Cars were his first and last love. They discussed how this could be turned to his advantage. Selling cars was a thankless occupation. But buying and selling vintage cars, special or rare cars . . . searching for them, the lure of the hunt and the sweet joy of reclamation and repair, of putting something old and broken back into shining circulation, was that not possible, something amusing, absorbing, to do?

Honoré, when the idea was put to him by Mrs Frampton, became alertly interested. They took to the road and almost at once found a large, level piece of ground between the farm and the sea, adjacent to a filling station and repair shop for sale. The road was a minor road, so business had been slow. But the facilities were there, and the workshop could be enlarged and the backing field, of poor land value, leased for a small sum.

Cars became the sole topic of conversation, and one evening, after a fervent discussion about Bugatti as a designer, Mrs Frampton found her hand gripped over the table ardently.

'You have done so much for me.'

'Nonsense.'

'You are so unselfish, I don't deserve.'

And suddenly, without warning, they were talking of May. For the first time, the forbidden subject, the dark lake of sadness that had threatened to engulf them both, was illumined, visible. Capable of traverse. They talked deep into the night. He told her of his first meeting with Little May, of seeing her on the steps of the Paris opera house as he waited to pick up a friend. He had got out of his car and asked her where she wished to go. And without pause, her own car to hand, she had got into his and they had gone to an hotel. Their love had been inexplicable and instantaneous. She had been, he said, like his own precious doll. A creature from another planet, a new, better species. He had learned to be gentle from necessity, trembling with clumsiness at her fragility. She had changed his life. She had taught him about painting, about literature, which he had been bored by in his youth. She had taught him about money. In turn, he had loved her, he had protected her, he had made her laugh during her days of remoteness, which he had diagnosed accurately as depression. He had become her eyes and ears. Mrs Frampton retold the story of the meeting of herself and Little May, when the *maître d'* on the beach had ordered the injured dog to be killed. How Mrs Frampton had picked up the poor creature and how this slight figure had stepped forward. How together they had watched the vet reset the dog's leg and stitch its wounds.

Honoré said, 'And I carried the dog to the car. A good dog.'

'Fortunato. I must ask the nuns how he is.'

'Not intelligent, not like Patrice.'

'No, but good natured.'

It was wonderful. They were able to talk about it. About May's childlike wonder, her sophistication, her occasional ruthlessness, her grace. They agreed . . . Honoré for the first time . . . that the accident had not been his fault. The other driver, who had swerved across the road, setting off the deadly train of collisions, had survived. He had been young. And drunk. He had confessed his fault, and was still imprisoned. No one, no one could have foreseen that moment. Honoré had done what he could. He had risked his own life, risked the car exploding, had been thrown back by it. The fact that he was alive was a miracle.

They spoke of their griefs, even of their guilt at being pleased to be alive.

'You've suffered,' said Mrs Frampton, stroking his scarred hand gently.

A little later he cried and put his head in her lap like a child. Then they went up to bed and he came into her room and made love to her as gently and as sweetly as she had ever known. They lay together for the rest of the night, murmuring and talking and playing together. His body, in the low light of the lamp, had never looked so beautiful. She wanted to draw him then and there – why had she never thought of painting him before? In the morning she would prime a canvas.

Early next morning, lying at her side, he said, 'You have given me back my life. We shall always be friends, shall we not?'

'I hope so.'

She was sleepy.

'And you will be happy for my happiness?'

'Yes, of course.'

She puzzled for moment, half awake.

'How do you mean exactly?'

With excitement, he leaned up on his elbow and kissed her forehead. And told her that he was going to marry Louise, the pale Louise, Madame Angelier's granddaughter.

Chapter 18

O H DEAR, THOUGHT Mrs Frampton as the steward opened
the cabin door and the other woman looked up and called
a loud hello. Obviously an American. To defer the moment she
ducked her head and rooted in her handbag for a tip.

'Will francs be all right?'

'Thank you, madam.'

'Are you kidding?' said the woman with whom she was to
share a cabin for five days. 'Francs, dollars, who cares, those
guys are dealers. The name's Caprice.'

She held out a hand with nails so long that they left incisions
in Mrs Frampton's palm.

'Sorry?'

'Caprice. Caprice di Hudson. Of course, when I picked it
out I didn't know the guy's orientation.' This was followed by
a low bellowing laugh which might not have been unpleasant
with fewer decibels and without the yell at the end. 'I mean,
in those days, who did? Then . . . after . . . I thought: Caprice,
what are you talking about, his orientation is the same as your
own, so what the hell!' She contemplated Mrs Frampton's blank
expression. 'Rock, honey. Rock Hudson.'

'The film star?'

'Guess his luck ran out, eh? Beautiful hairline.'

Mrs Frampton, baffled, began to unpack her things on the
corner of the bunk uncluttered by what looked like the wardrobe
for a musical comedy. Orienteering? What had Rock Hudson got
to do with mountain climbing?

She groaned inwardly. One highly expensive suite had been
vacant when her travel agent had telephoned. She had said yes
at once but it had been gone by the time the connection was

101

remade. The only vacancies, available through cancellation, were in two- or four-berth cabins.

Trust me to land a dud, she thought, warily watching the other woman disappear into the shower. She sat on the bed. Never mind. Think nothing about it. At least I have a table to myself.

She sat through dinner in a daze. The journey had been so sudden, so unprepared, that her mind was in a muddle. What had she packed? Did it matter? In any case there were shops on board selling clothes and toiletries, as she had discovered on a pre-dinner prowl. There was a cinema and a library and a theatre, with a series of talks listed. To her surprise, her cabin companion's name was down as a speaker, though the title 'Yesterday, Today and Tomorrow' gave little away. Perhaps she was a romantic novelist, that would explain the lush dresses and bead jackets.

I suppose I'll have to go.

Her spirits lifted slightly at the awfulness of her neighbours. At the nearer table eight Americans brayed sonorously, their nasal tones unmodified by the proximity of fellow passengers. Both men and women, crisp and fresh and laundered (how?), wore pale cashmere, and fawn trousers and skirts. Even their faces were fawn. Five Englishmen were at the other table. Their tones, too, rang with forced, jovial resonance. Mrs Frampton, her mind flickering on her years as a businessman's wife in Bradford, watched with fascinated loathing.

At least I'm out of that.

Without appetite, she sat until the steward removed her plate, and stayed sipping coffee, shy of crossing the animated dining-room. A shadow loomed.

'Hey,' said Caprice di Hudson. 'What are you doing all by yourself? Don't tell me they put you in this squitty corner by the service door?'

'I wanted a single.'

Mrs Frampton looked up into a pair of amazing blue orbs. The woman must be wearing contacts, nobody's eyes were that blue. Her teeth, too, pristine white, must be capped.

'I've just finished,' said Mrs Frampton, rising to make her escape.

'Come on. You need a drink.'

Mrs Frampton was not displeased to have a companion in the bar. Alone, you were horribly self-conscious. She allowed the American to buy her a brandy.

'D'ya smoke, May?'

'No, I don't.'

'Good, because I don't allow it around me. You can get the Big C.'

'By breathing other people's smoke?'

'Passive smoking, yeah – gee, when you think about it, air's recycled all the time . . . I'm probably breathing what just came out of that fat guy over there, oh my God.'

Despite herself, Mrs Frampton chuckled briefly.

'What do you know? You're feeling better already – right?'

Mrs Frampton, startled, flashed the woman a quick glance. Damn. Who does she think she is? Because we're sharing a cabin doesn't make her my bosom friend. If she's not careful I'll flag down that steward and order twenty Players.

'How was your dinner?' asked Caprice di Hudson.

'I had some salmon. I wasn't very hungry, actually.' To cover the slight silence she asked unwillingly, 'What did you have?'

'Calf's liver. Yuch, I hate it.' Mrs Frampton frowned enquiry. 'I never touched liver till a year ago, I just knew I wouldn't enjoy it.' Miss, or Mrs, di Hudson sighed – it was impossible to gauge her state since most of her fingers were heavily endowed with what seemed to be genuine diamond rings, one a handsome art deco knuckleduster.

'Then . . .'

'I order it so's I won't eat anything. Better than spewing up after, the stomach acid can play hell with your teeth.'

Again Mrs Frampton was lost. This woman talked a different language.

A tall, emaciated girl approached, teetering on narrow heels.

'Miz di Hudson, did you want to read this over, listen, I'm sorry I – '

'Sit down, Ruby . . . Ruby Merck, my assistant . . . May Frampton, my new cabin mate.'

'I tried, Mrs di Hudson.' Oh, so she was a Mrs. 'First I saw the assistant purser, he said to see the purser, who was remote, then would you believe it I broke my bra strap and then these girls lost their shoes so I gave them directions and this . . . man remonstrated with me for being in the wrong area. Mrs di Hudson, I'm sorry about the tickets.'

'Why are you wearing a bowler hat?' asked Mrs di Hudson. 'Never mind,' she added kindly. 'Leave the papers with me and go and dance. It will be good for the problem with your ankle.'

They watched Ruby go.

'Are you sure?' asked Mrs Frampton.

'It isn't entirely her fault,' said Caprice di Hudson. 'We had a bad time in Frankfurt. I was doing a makeover on this woman and she starts screaming because she had asked for a Sigourney Weaver, I told her, the nose, you should fix the nose, but she said she already had, and, you guessed, Ruby asked why did you accept it, we're gonna have to sue for the fee.' She waved a hand. 'Waiter, honey, freshen this up for me would you – with a twist.' She turned to Mrs Frampton with a beaming smile. 'Why should you listen to my troubles? Drink up and tell me your life.'

Mrs Frampton, awash with the other woman's voice, was stumped.

'I . . . I have a son in America. He's working in Boston. I'm on a visit.'

The woman's face seemed too close. For a moment Mrs Frampton felt a wave of acute nausea. She closed her eyes briefly. When she opened them Caprice di Hudson was regarding her steadily with her improbable blue eyes.

'I'm a bit tired,' said Mrs Frampton. 'I hadn't really planned on coming away.'

'Why was that?'

Again the woman's voice seemed slightly remote. Mrs Frampton took a breath, pulling herself together.

'Oh, nothing. I suddenly felt like a trip.'

Oh dear. I made a mess of that. What am I supposed to say? That my lover, who is nearly twenty years younger than me, has announced his engagement to a woman of twenty-eight? That I did a bunk overnight? That I picked up the *Queen Elizabeth* in Cherbourg by the skin of my teeth? That nobody knows where I am?

'Are you OK?'

The megaphone voice caused three heads to turn. Mrs Frampton said that she was fine, thank you, and added, 'I gather you had a rush yourself.'

'Are you kidding? What a movie scene! I thought I was the girl with the lashes who has to drive the aircraft with the hole in it and Charlton Heston's coming in on a rope, know what I mean – here, over here.' She grabbed her drink from the steward's tray as Mrs Frampton, wondering how she was going to survive the five days, maintained a decent silence.

'Listen,' said Caprice di Hudson. 'Why don't we two get smashed? I mean really float away?'

'I don't think I'm up to it,' said Mrs Frampton, shaking her head.

'Come on! Why not? The weather forecast is terrible, we're all going to be throwing up anyway, so what the hell?'

Chapter 19

As CAPRICE DI HUDSON had pronounced, the weather worsened. At first the sea grew grey and sluggish and then white horses, in the brief moonlight, made a Japanese painting of the wide view until darkness fell and there was only a misty wall. An awesome swell developed. Mrs Frampton, comatose with brandy, slept at first heavily, and then woke, and slept and woke and slept again with feelings of vague threat and a sense of loss, of dreams broken off, never to be rediscovered. At six forty-five she was woken by the sound of crashing china and went on deck, exhilarated by the high rolling surf and crashing waves. Spray, so hard that it smarted, dashed against cabin windows, and the decks, awash, were treacherous. She made for a sheltered corner out of the wind, by the rail.

'I shouldn't stay there if I were you, love!'

Mrs Frampton looked up as a deckhand shouted to her. She made to leave obediently but when he had gone returned to the rail by a lifeboat stanchion. The sea was magnificent. It didn't care! Nothing mattered to the sea. It surged and heaved and threw itself about . . . everywhere you looked there was nothing but chaos. What a rage. With wet hair she went below to the dining-room where the breakfast tables were almost empty. Of her neighbours only two Americans perused their menus in thoughtful silence and a single Englishman with a nutcracker face chewed firmly and wielded his coffee pot to creaks and grinds and occasional crashes. Mrs Frampton acknowledged his cordial wave and ordered a boiled egg. An hour later, wrapped in blankets by a solicitous steward, she was in a sheltered spot on deck once more.

How strange. There is nowhere else in the world I want to be. I just want to go on watching the water. Nothing else. Nothing and nobody.

I should send a message to Michael, tell them I'm coming. What if Chloe rings the farm? What would he tell her, the man whose name she could not bear even to mouth?

On the way to Paris she had sat by the misted window and it seemed, in a dream, as though he were her son, and that he had died. What nonsense. She had tried to pull herself together, but had gone to pieces, wanting to run about and take people by the arm, shout out her dreadful news. She bent over with the pain, remembering his answers to her stuttered questions.

'She is my type.'

His type!

After all that! All that effort . . . wasted! Better not to have been given the prince's kiss, never to have become acquainted with her whole self.

I never bothered about all that before, but now . . . now another creature had been given birth. They had given each other life. Well, we're quits. But they weren't. I'm left with nothing.

Useless thinking that she should be grateful for the long nights, the lazy mornings, the days of passionate talk. She had a new appetite, new needs that demanded. You ate, you slept, you peed and you made love. You did things with another person. Sometimes it was no more than a hand on the shoulder, a caress in passing, but you needed it. And how was she to find someone else? It was hopeless. It was totally hopeless because it was totally out of time. She should have been doing all this earlier in her life. A thought invaded.

Perhaps I should have stayed. Taken what I could get, the odd visit for old time's sake. Depended on his gratitude, his sexual amiability. She thought morosely: If I'd been a Frenchwoman I could have carried it off. I could have been his friend, his confidante – Who knows, the marriage might not even last!

She sat up firmly. No more of it. She took a walk round the wet decks and went below to buy an expensive black oilskin from a boutique. She was sipping Bovril on the afterdeck when Caprice di Hudson, aflame in red and yellow poncho and fisherman's hat, came at her with a tiptoeing run and was hurled into the seat beside her as the ship rode the waves.

'You look jolly,' said Mrs Frampton.

'Yup, the second officer offered to rent me a llama – does it ever end?'

'You've got me there,' said Mrs Frampton. And thought gloomily: She has me doing it now. For something to say she asked how Ruby was surviving the storm.

'Are you kidding? That kid wouldn't survive a trip to the john.'

'How old is she?' The dark Ruby looked far from a kid.

'God knows, but whatever it is she looks it.'

Mrs di Hudson rolled her eyes as the steward swooped with coffee and biscuits and slid off into the lap of an elderly Swede.

'Let me tell you, that woman is unemployable.'

'Then why – '

The blue eyes regarded her with their odd calmness.

'What is she going to do, sell her body? Who'd take it?'

Mrs Frampton, pondering on Ruby in her gaunt, black, bandage-tight dress, giggled. There was a companionable silence.

'Will you go to Boston directly?'

'I suppose so,' said Mrs Frampton, who had not made up her mind about anything. 'This is my first visit – I'd be glad of any tips. I mean, you think you know America from films, but I dare say that's misleading.'

'Yes and no,' said Caprice di Hudson. 'In one way it's exactly like the movies because that is where people get it from. You have to get it from somewhere.'

Get what? Mrs Frampton wondered. Caprice di Hudson, seeming to catch her inner drift, reared up from her recliner.

'Listen, babe. You think you're on a ship . . . on a boat? Wait till you hit the good old US of A . . . biggest ship in the world, I'm telling you. Moored right there in the middle of two damned great oceans. Some liner. I'll tell you, most of us wonder what the hell we're doing there most of the time. Well, bar the Indians, I guess, and they're in trouble.'

She lay back on the blue canvas cushion. Mrs Frampton, discerning an indigo mood in her companion, wondered if she was suffering a hangover. But the woman sat up, adjusting her outfit with expert fingers.

'Yeah, why not? Do some travelling. There's places to see. I can't tell you about Wyoming, Pittsburgh, places like that. I know Aspen, but my remit is the Coast – LA . . . and New York. And Florida, I have a place there. Hey, Cyril, I changed my mind.'

The steward, hearing her loud hail, arabesqued over skilfully with his tray.

'How's the back?'

'Oh, much better, thank you, Mrs di Hudson.' He bent and whispered confidentially in her ear. 'I did as you said.'

'Di'n' I tell you?'

'You've got them trained,' said Mrs Frampton as they sipped their coffee.

'Sure, you know why? Tip them at the start not the finish.'

At lunch, in the half-empty dining-room, they sat together.

'See that guy? That's Pierre de Rey. Ex-diplomatic. His wife was a well-known you-know-what.'

Mrs Frampton craned discreetly for a glance at Madame de Rey, a svelte woman with a smoothed face, whose scent knocked you out as she passed. Caprice di Hudson leaned over the table.

'One of the best in her line. They can make good marriages, especially with older men.'

Mrs Frampton, possibly due to the wine they were having with their fish, or perhaps not to be left behind, revealed her past as a nurse, and the problem of dealing with men's desires when they were flat on their backs.

'What did you do, did you . . . you know . . . keep them happy?'

'No, I didn't,' said Mrs Frampton, and for the first time in her life thought: Why didn't I? At least the ones I fancied . . . or the poor ugly ones, or the ones who weren't going to make it. Oh, how silly. I just never thought.

'An awful lot of men marry the nurse,' said Caprice di Hudson. 'Did you marry a patient?'

'Me? No. I married a man who ran a machine shop. He did well for himself eventually.'

'He's dead?'

'Yes.'

'I'm sorry.'

'Oh, that's all right; I never liked him much.'

'Just the one? Marriage?'

'Yes. How about you?'

'Five . . . I think it's five. I misremember which ones I married sometimes. Lemme think, I've been Mrs Heller, Mrs Vacani, Mrs Corder – that was Jim Corder, he'd have been fine without the drinking problem . . . little Lewis, married him for the money . . . oh, what the hell . . .'

She threw back her head, stylishly bound in the scarf against the wind, displaying a fine column of a throat.

'You're not married now?'

'Nope. Have my own business.'

'What do you do, exactly?'

'You mean you never heard of me? You never read my books?' Mrs Frampton shook her head.

'You didn't read *Your Fabulous Forties* . . . *Your Fantastic Fifties*? My first book . . . *It's No Rehearsal, Folks!*?'

'I'm sorry, no.'

'You don't know me, then . . . you don't know who I am? Oh hell. I feel like Joan Fontaine in *Rebecca*.'

'I hope you're not putting me in as Mrs Danvers,' said Mrs Frampton.

Caprice di Hudson patted her hand and laughed loudly.

'Nah, you know what I mean. I just assumed you knew who I was; I always have my picture on the dustjacket.'

'You're a writer?'

'I write books. I lecture, I do videos. I act as consultant, for movies, management, people with problems, stress, that kind of thing.'

'Sort of pyschology?'

'Sort of everything,' said Caprice di Hudson darkly. 'Sort of life.'

'How did you get into it?'

'That,' said Caprice di Hudson, 'is a very long story. Are you sure you want to hear it?'

'No,' said Mrs Frampton, 'but the ship's too wobbly to do anything else.'

'And my lecture is cancelled. What say we make for that little bar with the cute barman?'

Chapter 20

'WELL, IF YOU blinked you wouldn't have seen me but I was in it and I had two lines to say,' said Caprice di Hudson. 'I had to say, "This way, Mr Parker," and then I had to say, "Thank you, Mr Parker, say hello to Mrs Parker." I did bigger parts but that was the only major movie. It's tough. They're coming up behind you all the time.'

Mrs Frampton, thrilled by listening to anecdotes of Hollywood, and to be sitting across from a woman who had met, so she affirmed, some of the most famous film stars in the world, nodded in sympathy.

'So you gave it up?'

'Not from choice. Anyway, you know how it is in your twenties . . . it's men, sex . . . I wanted children . . . that took an awful lot of time.'

'How many children do you have?' asked Mrs Frampton.

'I had a son, by my second husband, Joe Vacani, best make-up man in the business. We lost him. He died of leukaemia.'

'How old – '

'He was six years of age.'

Caprice di Hudson, it appeared, had been born Verleen Burgess in Burbank, California. It was, she said, contrary to what Mrs Frampton might think, the most awful place in the world. Just miles and miles of suburbs, with yes, plenty of amenities in terms of things like parks and air conditioning and car-wash facilities. Everybody worked in the movies or in silicon city, in electronics or the air industry. Her father had left when she was six and her sister Jayleen four. Her mother had married again but that marriage had not taken, and after that there were just uncles. Jayleen had married young and had four children, all girls, while Caprice, renaming herself Sandra

Bellman, and later Andrea Fisher, had become a dancer, and later a small-part actress. She had lived the wild world of the Sixties, she had believed in all of it, the astrology, the *Gestalt*, the rolfing and the breathing, the hatha yoga, the jogging and the crystals. Nowadays, she said, everything was mood. What mood am I in, do our moods fit, are we properly attuned to go to contract.

'I read that everybody took cocaine,' said Mrs Frampton.

'No, no,' said Caprice di Hudson. 'It's health now. Personal nutritionist, personal masseur, personal allergist . . . I have a friend who's making a bomb arranging marriages between people's pets . . . she reads their auras.'

'So you got into the racket?' asked Mrs Frampton, awash on her third brandy.

'Eventually. I was having a marvellous time with a guy called Frank Perthan. He was in nylon . . . He had factories, he was loaded, import, export, all over the world – he had very big interests in the Far East. We travelled everywhere together. We went to the Andes, we saw Alaska, we saw India, Africa . . . he had a charitable foundation there. We did everything. I was good for him, I made him laugh, I made him rest. I thought we were friends for the rest of our lives and he wasn't bad . . . you know . . . in the sack . . . I could stand him.'

'How old was he?'

'Late sixties. Here.'

She handed Mrs Frampton one of a sheaf of small photographs. Mrs Frampton looked at a short, fat, balding, elderly man. Caprice leaned over her shoulder.

'What do you want? The guy was rich and I was forty-two.'

'Did he die?'

'You kidding? We came back from a trip to Europe, he liked Italian opera, his name was Peritani really, I just get unpacked, we have this sweet place in Warren Heights when he comes into the bathroom and he says, with his toothbrush in his mouth, foam on the chin, hey, babe, no hard feelings but I'm trading you in for a younger lady – just for image, no hard feelings.'

'Did he leave you provided for?'

'No. Not at all. Over the years he bought me all sorts of stuff

– a pearl necklace, a beautiful brooch, sapphire ring, but when I went to the bank it was gone.'

'What did you do?'

'I'll tell you what I did. I looked in the mirror. I looked and I said to myself, Andrea, your lips are getting thin, you're too fat and you don't suit strawberry blonde any more.'

'So you – '

'I traded in my car and got a makeover. I went to a Chinese girl called Leoni. We became friends so I took a job with her.'

'Putting people together?'

'Yeah. I liked the work. In a funny kind of way, it's playing with dolls . . . you know, dressing people up, changing them, making them go to the gym, getting tough, being understanding. I found I was good at it. You hear some terrible stories.'

'I know,' said Mrs Frampton.

'Well, you would,' said Caprice di Hudson.

On the third day the weather eased and Caprice gave her lecture in the theatre. Since Ruby was still *hors de combat*, Mrs Frampton stood in, waiting in the wings with notes, a carafe and combs and pins for emergencies. From there she saw Caprice take over her audience. She squinted at the faces, men as well as women, as Caprice told them to live now, to take chances, to beat their nerves, their fears, told them that the world belonged to them, and they to the world.

It certainly seems to work, she thought, as the queue to buy the books reached out into the corridor after prolonged applause and handshaking.

'See what I mean?' said Caprice, as they recovered with a tray of coffee. She seemed exhausted. 'It takes a hell of a lot out of you.'

There was a bumping sound, and a woman in a wheelchair, so heavily spastic that she seemed to be a head on legs with no body in between, approached their corner in the lounge.

'I'm sorry,' she said. 'I don't want to intrude.'

'Not a bit,' said Caprice di Hudson. 'What do you need to know? I'm here to help.'

'It's clothes,' said the woman. Mrs Frampton sat silently as the handicapped woman, who said her name was Nora Jero, explained her problems.

'Simple,' pronounced Caprice, stalking round the wheelchair and perusing the little woman. 'Yeah.'

She sat down again, and gave the woman a coffee.

'Now listen. You have a very good skin. Good eyes, they're large. Go for the eye make-up, not blue or green, use shades of soft mauve and brown, even a little pink for evening. Thin your eyebrows here and here, to lift them. Change your hairstyle, your hairstyle is OK, but it's boring. Go for something more dramatic. Try a wig at first if you're chicken, it doesn't have to be an expensive one, just get the hairdresser to experiment with styles. Swoop it up each side of your face, you can have bangs if you want, and catch it up with combs so it's interesting, sort of like a Gustav Klimt painting. Now clothes. You have to go for neck interest. Work on that. Beautiful Pierrot collars, goffered linen, lace . . . become an expert in lace, Brussels, *pointe de Venise*, there are some stunning old collars on the market. Wear velvet, and jewels, pearls next to your skin, OK, it's a cliché but it works. You have to glow, make yourself feature. You have a good neck, good hair, good skin. You just need to put it all together. And use lovely, inky colours. There's something vibrant about you that needs bringing out. OK, so you're in the chair. That doesn't mean you can't impose your personality.'

The woman leaned forward and pressed Caprice's hand against her cheek for a moment and then turned the chair and went away. There was a silence. After which Caprice di Hudson honked in a braying voice for more coffee and made a fuss that it wasn't hot enough and was given yet another pot. She bent over the cups and turned to Mrs Frampton abruptly.

'OK, so what about you, where are you coming from? Thanks for helping out, by the way – for once I felt secure, it was great.'

'I enjoyed it,' said Mrs Frampton truthfully. It had been satisfying to have something to do, a job. She was going to miss Caprice di Hudson. They always said it happened on sea voyages. You got close to people, swore to meet.

We'll exchange addresses, I dare say. And that will be that.

'What about you?'

'I'm sorry?'

'You haven't told me a thing about yourself.'

'There's nothing to tell. I've led a very ordinary life.'

'Then how come – ?' Caprice di Hudson, sipping her coffee, looked at Mrs Frampton's face and shut up. There was silence for a while between them. They lay back, listening to the noises of the boat. From below, somewhere, came the thrum of music.

'Are you on the run?'

'Yes. Yes, I suppose you could say that.'

'Do you want to talk about it?'

'Not in the least.'

There was silence again. Caprice di Hudson, to Mrs Frampton's surprise, dived into her bag, took out a gold cigarette case, and lit up.

'I didn't know you smoked.'

'Just rarely, but it's so wonderful in the fresh air.'

She drew on the cigarette a couple of times and then stubbed it out. Then she said, very quietly, 'You don't think that talking about it would do something for the pain?'

'No, I don't,' said Mrs Frampton.

Chapter 21

O N THE LAST morning Mrs Frampton booked a radio telephone
call to her son Michael. When she came back to the saloon to
join Caprice di Hudson at the bar her face conveyed disappointment.

'What is it?'

'He's not there, they're not there. Silly of me, they didn't
know I was coming, of course.'

Caprice di Hudson ordered two large Camparis.

'They've let their house to friends for three months.'

'Three months? Where are they?'

'Tokyo. Michael is giving lectures. Then they're going to
Australia to see Stephanie's people. I remember now, they
said.'

'Perhaps you could catch up with them.'

Mrs Frampton found that idea entirely too much for her. She
explained that, unlike her companion, she was unused to world
travel.

'What will you do?'

'I don't know. Return on the ship, I suppose, if they have a
place for me.'

Caprice di Hudson ate a handful of peanuts.

'I wouldn't do that.'

'Why not? I've nothing to – '

'Come up on deck.'

They got their coats, for the weather was colder, and went
up to the top deck together. For two hours they stood as the
New York skyline emerged from the haze.

'Look,' said Caprice di Hudson, 'the Statue of Liberty.'

'But it's so much bigger than in the films and photographs!'

'You can't just go home,' said Caprice di Hudson. 'You'd

never forgive yourself and that's the hardest thing to do in any situation.'

'You think I should do the grand tour?'

'I can think of worse ideas. Listen, you don't have to make up your mind right away, you can always take a plane. Come and stay in the apartment, you'll like it, it's kind of European – I'm a fool for all that stuff.'

Mrs Frampton protested.

'Don't think about it – there are five bedrooms, we'll never see each other. You can take a look at New York.' She gestured at the unbelievable skyline in the weak morning sun. 'I have to go and find Ruby, see how many bags she's left in Europe and which capital city hosts our passports, I don't doubt. And don't get hassled about customs. They're rude, rude, rude. Expect it, you won't be surprised. Stay close, I have a car.'

In the event, customs were surprisingly cordial. Ruby, as expected, had mislaid both papers and baggage, so there was delay, mostly while she explained that she was menstruating, and in any case, that her father preferred her brother. Mrs di Hudson seemed to take this with calm, rather than cracking the girl over the head, which Mrs Frampton soon felt like doing. But was placated by the car which awaited them, an immense pale silver limousine with a sedate black driver called Bob, who welcomed his employer with a hug and who took over the three women with protective care. Sitting behind his broad shoulders, Mrs Frampton felt easier. She twisted her head this way and that and Caprice di Hudson let down the silent windows so that she might gaze out and up at the canyons of skyscrapers.

'This is Fifth Avenue?'

She gawped. Never had she seen so many fur coats. Men as well as women wore mink coats, wolf jackets . . . Was that sable?

'Is that sable?'

'You're not kidding,' said Caprice di Hudson.

'Fur coats belong on animals,' said Ruby.

The apartment was on the ground floor with a small courtyard at the back, a precious open space planted in the French style with small trees and shrubs grown for contrasting leaf colours and shapes, and a few stone urns festooned with ivy. Inside, the rooms were vast, furnished with pale rugs and sofas, and modern paintings. She stood before a large oil of a demented woman.

'De Kooning?'

'Crazy guy, eh?'

There was a dining-room with a glass table and mobiles, an enormous music room with white piano, white carpet and gold chairs, and several capacious bedrooms . . .

'Use this one,' said Caprice di Hudson. 'It gets the morning sun. Freshen up and we'll go to lunch.'

The bedroom was large with a walk-in closet and a bathroom so sybaritic that Mrs Frampton slid at once into the vast, deep tub and lay back in ecstasy, feeling the tension leave her shoulders. What a piece of luck! Caprice must be very rich to afford such a palace. You could almost float in the bath, and, as for soap, there were large Lalique glass bowls full of it, and stacks of face flannels and towels, enough for a platoon . . .

I feel as if I'm in ancient Rome!

She wrapped herself in a towelling robe and dried her hair.

I almost feel hungry!

On board the ship her appetite had remained as it had been in Paris. In vain had the stewards leaned over her with plump trout, lobster, tournedos and luscious puddings. They had not been able to make her out, a passenger who arrived for all her meals, even during the storm, but who ate nothing.

At least my weight is well down.

The trouble was that her chin sagged and there were new lines from nose to mouth which gave her a doleful look. Talk about reading the face. She gazed at herself in the art deco mirror, removing all expression.

Oh dear. There was nothing there. No one at home. Well, that's the truth of it. All thinking had had to cease. No thought being tolerable, no thought was permitted.

She drew back from the mirror and made a face at herself. An unpleasant face. Yes, that was more like it. A witch. Witches were dangerous people.

I'll have to watch it.

They walked out on to Columbus Avenue and into a green-and-white restaurant with shining girls in pink aprons.

'What about Ruby?'

Mrs di Hudson frowned and shook her head.

'Are you kidding? The fridge is full of food, organic, schmorganic, she won't starve, course there won't be a thing she likes and she'll drive Luisa crazy . . . you didn't eat with her, did you? She treats every waiter in New York like the mother she is not going to please, it gets to you . . . Try the pan-fried chicken, or the broiled scrod is good.'

A lustrous girl in high-heeled boots swayed towards them with a caring smile.

'Good morning, ladies. Today our specials are . . .'

Mrs Frampton, embarrassed and slightly irritated, fidgeted while the girl reeled off a long list of dishes that were already written up on a blackboard over the serving hatch.

'What was all that about?' she whispered, as the girl returned with a large pitcher of iced water. 'We *can* read.'

'It's the custom,' said Caprice di Hudson, demolishing a breadstick. 'A lot of these girls are out-of-work stage people. They like to impose themselves.'

'It's an imposition, all right,' grumbled Mrs Frampton. Caprice di Hudson, who had a slight gap between her surprisingly uncapped teeth, grinned her fox's grin.

'This is a tough city – you have to draw attention to yourself.'

'Which part is this?' asked Mrs Frampton, who had no idea where she was, and was not particularly bothered.

'Central Park West. It's sort of like the Left Bank, Covent Garden, maybe. The Lincoln Centre is here . . . opera, ballet, legitimate theatre . . . just down the road aways.'

'Is that why everyone you see has an instrument case?'

'Either that or they walk like ducks.'

As she spoke, two swan-necked girls passed the window.

'See what I mean? Shall we share a bottle of red?'

The wine, Spanish, was inky and fiery at once, and surprisingly potent. Caprice became expansive. She sent a waitress out for a map of New York and pointed out the areas: Manhattan, Bronx, Queen's . . . SoHo, Greenwich Village, the lower east side, the park. Mrs Frampton, becoming drunk, asked polite questions and feigned interest. Caprice di Hudson, infected with her role as historian, waxed eloquent. Which made her thirsty and demand liqueurs with their coffee.

Reeling out into the crisp, invigorating air, they decided to walk in the little park across the street which backed the Natural History Museum. After a number of traverses they sat down, enjoying the late-autumn sun, and Caprice di Hudson spoke of her plans. She was about to leave New York for a national speaking tour.

'And after that take off . . . maybe the snow, maybe Florida. I have a new book to write, but who cares? I'll be tired, I'll take a rest, spend the fees . . . maybe look for an adventure.'

'An adventure?'

'Things happen.'

'Do they?'

Caprice di Hudson turned to look at her.

'Yes. If you wish them to.'

'Not to all of us. Most of us are here for the chores. We're allowed to look, see what we can't have.'

'You're depressed.'

There was a silence. This was the first time the word had been spoken between them. Mrs di Hudson fidgeted for a moment, pulling at her gloves. She turned and looked at Mrs Frampton.

'You've had a knock, haven't you?'

'I can't even think.'

'That bad?'

'I daren't.'

'Then take your time.'

'The trouble is . . .' said Mrs Frampton. 'The trouble is, it happened too late for me. The older you get, the deeper it . . .' She paused and picked up an old crust of bread and threw it at the pigeons. 'It took me flat aback. I don't know how to cope.'

'Look,' said Caprice di Hudson. 'I have three engagements here in Manhattan then I'm on the road till Christmas. Why don't you come along? You might as well and I need the help. You're the helpingest woman I've met for years; it would be a luxury to leave Ruby in the office.'

'Why don't you fire her?'

'I know. I should. Listen, it would make her happy, she hates travelling, she says it gives her hives, and she keeps sniffing things . . . sprays and stuff. Drives you crazy.'

'I don't know,' said Mrs Frampton, feeling suddenly flat as the wine began to wear off.

'What have you got to lose? Your family aren't back until the New Year, why not see something of this great continent? You'll be amazed, I promise. Take a chance . . . why not?'

'I'll think about it.'

Chapter 22

'CAPRICE!' YELLED MRS FRAMPTON. 'Caprice! They're waiting for you, you're on!' She ran up the narrow stairs to the dressing room as Caprice emerged in her gold sheath and silver cap.

'How do I look?'

'Stunning.'

She flattened herself against the wall for Caprice to pass. The little hat curved about her skull; it was a success, they had been right to buy it. There had been a scare with the lights, but the man had put in pink gels.

She doesn't look a day over thirty-five on the rostrum.

In the dressing room the theatre dresser, Min, was hanging up Caprice's street clothes.

'She looks wonderful, Min.'

'Thanks, Miz Frampton. You going down?'

'You bet. Give me her things.'

Min had the tray, with the powder and hairbrush and comb. There was an Evian spray and a box of pins, needles and cotton for instant repairs. Mrs Frampton tiptoed carefully down the winding, narrow stairs and took up her position on the prompt side, as she now knew to call it, in the wings. Not all of the engagements were in theatres but Mrs Frampton particularly enjoyed these. The atmosphere was different from the civic halls, hotels and convention spaces. The theatres were places of imagination. Often rubbed and old and in need of repair, their walls still sang. She felt at home in them. There was a strange atmosphere of understanding. You felt lighter.

She listened to the applause dying away, and heard Caprice's opening words. She was changing her format tonight . . . how brave! She risked herself. This was a huge auditorium, a special occasion, part of a five-day state-wide charity appeal. Tonight's receipts were in aid of leukaemia patients and, as a well-known patron, Caprice was giving her services free. It was the last engagement of the tour and she was in festive mood, calling volunteers on to the stage and telling jokes, leaving her prepared text altogether and turning the evening into a wonderful party.

How could she do it! Mrs Frampton stood, hands clasped, with tears of wonder in her eyes, waving back as Caprice grinned at her merrily. Who would believe it to look at her now, shining and witty and beautiful? All day she had fiddled about and half an hour ago she had whined in the dressing room like a frightened child. Catching Mrs Frampton's eye, she had smiled her wolf smile, but with a grim mirthlessness. As Min had buttoned her sleeves, she shook, and they had had to repowder her face as the sweat came through. Who would believe it now?

At the reception they were fêted. It took a long time to get away, but at last they left the air-conditioned rooms, followed by farewells, into the steam heat of Tampico. Their luggage was already packed in the rented car, which was waiting to take them down the coast. This was to be the last jaunt before they returned to New York. Soon Caprice was bound for Aspen and then Hawaii, where she would tape her new book. Mrs Frampton would make her way to Boston. They climbed into the cool of the car, where the young driver said his name was Jeff.

'Make it smooth, Jeff,' said Caprice. 'We need a nice easy ride.'

'You bet, Mrs di Hudson,' he said, letting in the clutch and grinning over his shoulder. Mrs Frampton, the cares of the evening dropping away from her, put a hand on Caprice's arm.

'Now are you going to tell me?'

Caprice di Hudson had been mysterious about the next and last port of call. She had taken a look at Mrs Frampton in Chicago and announced her intention of treating her new, unpaid assistant to a holiday at the end of the tour.

'I keep telling you – trust me.'

124

Mrs Frampton sank back on the cool plastic seat.

I should trust her. She's a winner. I hope it's nowhere too grand, I haven't the clothes. What does it matter? I'll just do as she says, live in the moment. Go here, go there. No thinking, that's the main thing. Take it as it comes, May.

She was awoken by a change in sound, and sat up with a jump. The car was going across a causeway, it seemed for miles. She struggled upright and looked out of the window. Serene water rippled gently in the riding lamps of boats and strings of lights from the shore behind them. Ahead was land and the dark, blurred shapes of trees.

'Where are we?'

But Caprice seemed to be dozing. She murmured something that could have been, Shut up. Mrs Frampton settled back in her seat as, on land again, the car turned right and droned almost silently along unlit roads. She opened a window and there was the scent of flowers. Now the car slowed almost to a halt to cross water over a modest bridge. No lights at all now, and then a few, from houses beyond trees, then more sweeping groves of casuarinas in the headlights. Suddenly the car swung into a driveway and a moment later pulled up before a house. A house in the air, high on stout wooden piles, as you saw in pictures of the South Seas.

'Come on,' said Caprice di Hudson, now seemingly wide awake. She marched up the wide wooden stairway, took out a bunch of keys, opened the door and ushered Mrs Frampton inside.

'Welcome to Grouper Creek.'

Mrs Frampton, moving from the open hallway to the long room beyond, walked its length to the terrace windows and looked out towards water.

'That's the sound. The ocean's the other side of the island.' She took off her linen jacket, threw it on a vast sofa covered with cushions, and turned to Mrs Frampton.

'Well, here we are.'

'Where are we?'

'On an island.'

'A desert island?'

Caprice di Hudson laughed her loud, barking laugh.

'Yeah . . . marooned. You'll see. Let's have some tea.'

They went into the kitchen, which had dark wooden walls, and made tea, and coffee for the driver for his journey back to Tampico.

'We'll hire a buggy tomorrow, show you around.'

'I'm going to fall asleep any minute.'

Mrs Frampton allowed herself to be steered to her bedroom, and nodded good-night and cleaned her teeth, noticing nothing. It had been a long day. They had come from Houston and before that there had been Detroit and Louisville and Chicago and Tallahassee and . . . where? She shook her head wearily, climbing between cool sheets. Not to mention tonight, and the reception after, with the sound of the salsa band on the terrace colliding with the strains of the jazz trio in the main hall. And everyone shining and glistening in harsh colour, and noise such as you never heard . . . with Caprice di Hudson, now in acid-lime sequins, fêted and yelling and screeching with the rest of them. As sleep descended she wondered where she was.

Never mind. I'm too tired to be curious. Anyway, who cares?

Chapter 23

T HE ROOM SEEMED full of light. Mrs Frampton sat up abruptly. Where was she? It took a full minute to come to. She looked around the room at dark-blue painted furniture, at the green coverlet on her bed. She slid out, her feet finding a rush mat, then a cool floor, and found the bathroom, and then crossed back to her open window for a look. A pelican flapped away. Overhead, huge palms dipped over the house and further off leaned towards one another, framing the water of the sound.

'Are you up?' called Caprice di Hudson.

'Yes!'

Before her were two more houses and another to her right. And then casuarina trees, a dark feathery green barrier. Ahead was the water. There was a small pier and a flagpole. A man in a blue hat was fishing from the pier and as she watched there was a silvery flashing glint in the sky as he lifted a fish from the water. The smell of coffee came from the kitchen. Mrs Frampton put on her dressing gown and walked through to the main room. Caprice was now on the terrace, leaning over the breakfast table.

'Are those hibiscus?'

Caprice di Hudson lifted the jug with the red and yellow blossoms.

'I just picked them.'

'Red and yellow,' said Mrs Frampton. 'Spanish colours.'

'Did you grow them in Spain?'

'Yes. I grew the double ones . . . pale-pink and buff . . . very beautiful but not as vigorous as the singles.'

Caprice di Hudson's blue eyes were on her. Then she bent and sniffed.

'No smell,' she said, pulling a face.

'No,' said Mrs Frampton. 'No smell.'

It was the first time she had made mention of her previous life unprompted.

After they had finished breakfast Mrs Frampton picked up her plate and cup, rising.

'No, leave it . . . there's a maid service.'

'Oh, I see. Did she stock the refrigerator?'

'No, that was Lil. She and Art built these houses . . . that's theirs by the pier, the larger house. He made a fortune in steel someplace and they used to come here to catch the kingfish. One year they didn't go back . . . Do you have your swimsuit?'

In Houston, at Caprice di Hudson's insistence, she had bought cotton dresses, shady hats and two swimming costumes, all in gaudy colours, there being none other on offer.

'I'm going to look like a fruit salad,' she had grumbled.

'Great, you'll fit in.'

'How do you mean?'

'You'll see,' Caprice had said.

As they trod carefully down the open wooden steps Lil Kellogg approached and Caprice, with an ear-damaging shriek, leapt the last steps and embraced her. Lil Kellogg was wearing blue-and-white sandshoes and striped socks on the end of long, craggy legs, pink-and-green-and-yellow shorts and a purple top with appliquéd cream-and-orange chrysanthemums. Together with a large straw hat with a black-and-white-checked bandanna, which she wore slung between her shoulder blades, and obviously did not use since her face was a deep, gingery brown and her neck and upper chest wrinkled by years of exposure to the sun. Caprice made the introductions.

'Where are you guys headed?'

'The beach.'

'First time?' asked Lil Kellogg, creasing a smile at Mrs Frampton.

'She hasn't seen a thing,' said Caprice di Hudson. 'We arrived late last night.'

'Everything OK?'

'Yeah . . . thanks, Lil.'

'My pleasure.'

They watched the tall, spidery figure lope off out of the drive. Mrs Frampton gawped after the day-glo apparition and turned to speak. Caprice di Hudson laughed.

'You'll get used to it.'

They left the compound of seven houses and walked out on to the sandy, unmade road. After a little way Caprice pointed and they crossed the road and turned down a shady path. At the end was the glint of the sea.

'The Gulf,' said Caprice di Hudson.

'The Gulf?'

'The Gulf of Mexico. I got to hear of this place from my dentist. I was having a bridge fixed and it was really slushy weather in New York, and my voice was in bad shape from a tour . . . Anyway, he said this was where the dentists came, and the doctors from the Mass General, and they're really, you know, the aristocracy – Harvard, you know. The great thing is it's all national park north of here, so there's no development on the other islands.'

They swung past two small frame houses and the ground became not dirt but a mixture of earth, pine needles and crushed shells.

'Here we are.'

They were on the beach, a long, white, dazzling strip which went as far as the eye could see, both ways. And ahead, the sea. A sea such as Mrs Frampton had never known, with colours that she seemed never to have seen before. A sea that looked like a smooth endless sheet of shot silk. There was blue, there was pink, there was green and grey, even a pure-yellow sheen, far out, beyond a single white fishing boat. Shocked by the suddenness, and feeling strange in the head, she could find nothing to say. There was a feeling somewhere, something that was trying, distantly, to be born. Was it gratitude? To this woman, this . . . this wise, noisy macaw of a woman who had taken the trouble to bring her here?

'Let's swim,' said Caprice di Hudson. 'It's absolutely safe. There's no current or undertow at all; you don't have to worry.'

But Mrs Frampton was gazing down at her feet, and all around her.

129

'Shells!'

'Yes,' said Caprice di Hudson. 'The beach is all shells. It's famous – one of the famous shell beaches of the world. That's why those people down there with pails all have their asses in the air. Collecting's a very big thing here.'

Mrs Frampton, seeing a pale flash of colour, bent and picked up a shell. It was exquisite, a small bowl, brown-and-white on the exterior, inside a chalky white with a centre of pure pink. Carefully she put it in the side pocket of her beach bag.

The feel of the water, too, was like silk. She swam out, calling back to Caprice, who stayed nearer the shore and became alarmed, that she was fine, that she was a strong swimmer.

I'll swim out to the boat, she thought, but it was further than it looked, and in any case it was hardly sensible to disturb the fish for the anglers. She lay on her back and floated.

Now I am really somewhere else. Elsewhere. Nowhere. In a paradise of nowhere. A lotus land, where everything is different. Different trees, different flowers, different plants. Everything to be discovered. I am in Florida, where the oranges come from. Where there are crocodiles.

She had seen films of Miami, with beaches crammed with hotels, and programmes on the crime, the drug-trafficking, on the problems of immigrants, of Cuban refugees. There had even been a jokey piece on Palm Beach, where all the aged residents were multimillionaires and you couldn't join the tennis club if you were Jewish. This place was nothing like that. Here, people hardly wore shoes.

Where am I?

She flopped over, getting water in her nose, and began a leisurely crawl back to the beach.

As she waded in and stood, gazing up and down the long strand, she thought to herself: Hello, there's a bit of a change here – I'm feeling alert.

It was probably the swim.

They walked up the beach to the top of the island. Here there were more stilted houses, large, with wide decks and awnings and lawns with sprinklers giving directly on to the beach.

'These are very fancy.'

'Prices to match,' said Caprice di Hudson. She led the way through to a large, immaculate garden complex which was the main hotel. Here they drank fruit juice and for half an hour played with space invaders, which were new to Mrs Frampton.

'You could get stuck into this, Caprice.'

'They're a disease.' Caprice jerked her head at the young lad next to them whose head had been down when they arrived and who was still playing the same machine when they left. By the small pier a passenger boat was moored.

'Where is the boat going?'

'Across the sound. There's an island which is privately owned that has some great houses. Shall we take a trip?'

'I'm game.'

'So that's the ocean over there, and this is the sound?' said Mrs Frampton as the boat chugged off between old wooden piles. 'What are the birds sitting on top of all the stakes?'

'Ospreys . . . sea eagles,' supplied the old man opposite. 'They're here for the fish.'

'Sure are,' said the pilot, turning the wheel and heading north.

The low sound of the boat made Mrs Frampton sleepy. She began, too, to feel hungry, and this was a feeling that had become so unfamiliar as to be momentarily alarming.

I feel like a good meal!

'Can we eat on this island?' she asked Caprice, who looked back at her with her blue-eyed stare.

'Sure can,' she said laconically, and began to whistle a Scott Joplin tune.

They passed several small islands and their fellow passenger, who said his name was Ed, and several other voyagers, intrigued by Mrs Frampton's accent, proffered information. The mangrove tree, said Ed, grew in salt water. Pretty soon its debris created a compost, seeds fell into it or were dropped by birds, and other plants grew, forming a new island.

'Till the damn hurricane comes along, knocks everything flat,' grumbled an old girl in a bright-yellow yachting cap.

There were murmurs of assent and the pilot described the

131

typhoon in the Twenties that had swept the island, destroying banana plantations for ever.

'It's the reason we're on stilts.'

There was an open passage of water, smooth but for the occasional plop of fish, and then the private island came into view, the sun glinting on its smart pier and dazzling white houses. Stepping ashore, Mrs Frampton felt she was stepping into a film. The houses with their white weather boarding and grey roofs were like something from Somerset Maugham.

I should be in a saggy white dress with a picture hat and a parasol.

'Let's eat,' said Caprice.

The clubhouse, it appeared, was one of the original houses on the island. There were photographs of the Roosevelt family and other notables who had come to fish, back at the turn of the century. Their pictures, lovingly framed in mahogany and burr-walnut, graced the bars and the large dining-room.

'There's a buffet on the lawn,' said the elegant girl who had come, in the now familiar style, to intone the dishes of the day.

Mrs Frampton followed Caprice di Hudson down the steps to a terrace where the food was laid out. She had never seen such a spread in her life . . . even the *Elizabeth* paled. Such lobsters! Monster crabs! And huge cut-glass dishes of mayonnaise, salads and side dishes and chicken, turkey, hams and roast beef, all shining and lustrous.

'Are you hungry?'

'My word,' said Mrs Frampton.

As they tottered, plates laden, to seats on the lawn, they were interrupted by a shriek. Caprice put down her plate and turned to be embraced by a large woman in long flowered shorts.

'Caprice di Hudson! Our first celeb. of the season . . .! Hi!'

'Inez! . . . How are you, where is everybody?'

'Well, the men, as they like to be called, are fishing for snapper, Dusty is here, and Céleste . . . she left Jack, by the way.'

'What? I thought she felt he was the best she could do for herself?'

'I know,' said Inez, sitting comfortably and eating celery from Mrs Frampton's plate. 'But it didn't work out. Like she said, if you don't want my apples, why shake my tree?'

'Oh, that's too bad.'

'It was OK till she said she wanted a baby – the guy made skid marks. Then the conditions started so she said what the hell and liquidised him. He's still making anonymous calls but that'll be useful for the settlement, I guess.'

They watched the large Inez roll away and thump up the steps.

'Nothing there money wouldn't cure,' murmured Caprice di Hudson professionally. 'You know, that woman knows Nixon . . . doesn't care for him, though.'

They ate prodigally and dozed in cushioned armchairs and then watched a bevy of children, the girls in bright dresses, the boys in frilled shirts, celebrate a birthday.

'What a shame,' murmured Mrs Frampton, looking at the children and then at the lush green grass and the swaying palms. 'Everyone should have this. It's not fair.'

'We're working on it.'

'Are we?'

Caprice di Hudson gave her a brief glance.

'Come on, let's walk, we have to sit on that boat for an hour.'

That evening, sleepy with food and fresh air, they sat out on the terrace with mint tea.

'Well? How are you feeling?'

'I seem to have changed planets,' said Mrs Frampton.

'Good.'

Chapter 24

S HE BOUGHT BOOKLETS on the local flora and fauna. They went to the larger island and shopped in exclusive boutiques on cleverly designed boardwalks with weathered wood.

'Sure it's pastiche,' said Lil Kellogg, 'but what do you want, tower blocks?'

Mrs Frampton, after spending far too much on a handkerchief-lawn dress with a wonderful asymmetric cut, felt that she had no right to want anything, ever again.

It's all so self-indulgent!

And yet. Through Lil she met Patti Steinberg, who lived in the compound and was a noted abstract expressionist. And who, when Caprice said she had never understood abstract expressionism, said, 'You understand Wagner, don't you . . .? You understand Beethoven . . . look!' And pointed up at the sunset which was a huge abstract, violet and pink and orange and crimson, right across the sky. They all laughed on her terrace, drinking violent blue cocktails which were not as lethal as they looked, thanks to Art Kellogg's passion for getting the thing right, as he called it.

They visited the local nature reserve and saw flocks of birds. And alligators, sleepy and still in the sun. One evening they sat for an hour on a neck of sand between the two islands waiting for the roseate terns to come in. Who had obliged them at last, feeding close by with their spooned bills and stained breasts. Some days they did nothing but lie on the beach and read. Mrs Frampton caught the shell fever, and bent and scavenged till her eyes swam, looking for treasures. She bought paper and crayons and began to draw. And noticed that her pictures were getting larger.

I wonder what that means. Perhaps I'd better be careful or I shall start to grow too big, like Alice.

Inside her heart, everything was locked safely away. Each bland, smiling day was a benison. Caprice went up to the hotel complex for her treatments, massage, mud baths, spot reduction and sauna, and Mrs Frampton, in a flurry of guilt, bought gifts for the family and had them gift-wrapped and despatched on her behalf.

She swam every morning, making acquaintance with other early risers . . . old Chuck who owned a bank in Idaho and who got such pleasure from goosing her that you couldn't take offence; Patti, who at seventy-three jogged up and down the hard wet sand for half an hour then swam a vigorous crawl that Mrs Frampton could not keep up with; Sandy and Jane, in their eighties, who floated and dabbled at the water's edge. They were avid shellers, exchanging treasures from their yellow buckets and drinking tots from lemonade bottles. They had known each other, they said, from childhood in upstate New York. They had seven husbands between them, eleven children, forty-seven grandchildren and eighteen great-grandchildren. Sandy's grandmother had trekked to California in a covered wagon. Both of them, according to Lil, were millionairesses many times over. What did they do with their money? asked Mrs Frampton. Oh, you know, said Lil, give it away. Mrs Frampton watched Sandy and Jane with interest. Neither of them wore so much as a watch. They disported themselves in the waves in faded bathing costumes and told mildly dirty jokes, drank their whisky and water and ate chicken legs and potato salad on the shore.

These people! So old – and so tough! Not an ounce of flesh on any of them. All of them with different recipes for longevity. You had to get away from cold climates. You had to keep the joints moving. You had to be interested in life. Not one of them ate the same diet, she noted. In one sense they were all self-centred. They did what they wanted and only what they wanted. They were like monstrous children. At the same time they still ran their affairs. Mr Low, their near neighbour, strode his lawn, phone hunched into his shoulder, instructing his stock broker on deals. Old Chuck, whose wife Polly was doing South America, received employees from his enterprises, arranging fishing parties for them, organising their days with paternal bossiness. Everyone stroked his bald head, the icon of their prosperity and security. He was their crusty old pappy but at the same time shrewd and tough. Not easily crossed.

They're amazing, all of them, thought Mrs Frampton. The successful ones. The ones who've clawed their way to the sun. Who look after themselves. The survivors.

Most amazing of all was Neet Olafsen. One morning, padding off for her early swim, Mrs Frampton had half-turned at a soft sound behind her and almost been clouted by a large bundle of clean laundry hurled from a golf cart on to the step of a small frame house. At the wheel of the cart was a lanky woman with white-yellow hair screwed into a knot, in faded khaki shorts and the usual garish cotton shirt in pink and green and purple.

'Hi, sorry, damn nearly got you, missed mah aim.'

'Do you need any help?' asked Mrs Frampton.

'Nope, finished.' She jerked her head to the small shack on the beach. 'The name's Neet . . . you going to breakfast?'

'I'll join you when I've finished my swim,' called Mrs Frampton, dodging the dirt as the golf cart spurted away.

Neet Olafsen (the Neet was short for Anita) was ninety-five. She was a full-time Floridian resident of Swedish stock who owned properties on the island which she rented to visitors. These, with little outside help, she serviced herself. Her family was spread over the globe, came to see her when they thought about it, she said. No, she wasn't much of a letter writer, couldn't remember how many grandchildren she had but was fond of one of them, name of Troy, a hell of a good kid and a great fisherman. Mrs Frampton watched Neet Olafsen eat her way through brittle, over-cooked bacon strips, waffles, eggs and link sausages, and drink two large mugs of black coffee before jolting off up the unmade road on her buggy.

It made you think. Here was a woman who appeared to live like a peasant – in a way they all did, but not really, she thought. Their lives were all based on highly complex support systems. Not so Neet. She might as well be back on the fjord. She saw to chores daily. She cleaned, organised changeovers, gardened, mended her small fishing boat herself, shopped at the

136

mall once a week in her old truck. She fed her dogs and bird, she minded animals for people, she forwarded mail, took in parcels, dispensed addresses, numbers and useful information. She seemed to be entirely content, the happiest human being that Mrs Frampton had ever met.

'Have you never been ill?'

The old woman had paused, squinted, and shaken her head. She was certainly old, and yet she wasn't. She was sharp and young, more like an adolescent.

I suppose it's a sort of second childhood, not in the meaning of senility, but in freedom, lack of responsibility. Yet she works like a slave and she can't have to.

On the terrace with Caprice and Lil Kellogg Mrs Frampton mused over her fruit cocktail.

'There must be something about this place, Shangri La or something – I mean, look at Neet Olafsen.'

'She's a stayer all right,' yelled Lil, with Caprice screeching in descant.

'Has she lived here all her life?'

'Nah.' Lil helped herself to a generous refill from the gigantic jug with the seahorses painted all over it.

'Nah. You never heard of Neet Olafsen?'

'Should I have?'

Caprice shrieked again, creasing up her fox's face.

'Did time for murder,' said Lil laconically, knocking back her fourth drink. Both of the women snickered joyously at Mrs Frampton's face.

'Mind you,' brayed Lil, 'they never proved it. Not incontrov . . . inconter . . . not absolut-damn-lutely. She got a five for manslaughter.'

'Who did she kill?'

'Who do you think?' bawled Caprice, who was on her third glass. 'Her old man, honey. Mind you, he was a shit.'

Mrs Frampton, offended by Lil Kellogg's turn of phrase, was silent. She was a good sort, Lil, but there was no need to drink the way she did. Caprice di Hudson took up the narrative. Neet had modelled clothes for Worth and Molyneux after winning beauty contests both locally and nationally. She

137

had married a South American and then a man who died in a flying accident.

'Was the next one Hal, Lilian?'

'Nah, the one after that. She did the right thing, knocking him off.'

'Why?' asked Mrs Frampton.

'They used to come here all the time when she was married to Jeff Ricardo. He was a nice guy, he was great with the kids.'

'How many children did she have?'

'Let me see, two boys with Romano, a daughter by Clifford, then she and Jeff had a little girl . . .'

'That makes four,' said Mrs Frampton, who had always yearned for a big family.

'Yeah, so then she meets Hal who's – you know – old money, lotsa style, which she likes, and old Jeffie's down there on Wall Street all the time making money to pay for the kids, so the next thing you know she's switched him for Big old Hal. With the mean streak. I knew his sisters, they came here a lot for the fish.'

'What were they like?' asked Caprice.

'Oh, same thing, plenty of style, that family.' Lil, having emptied the jug, took uncomplainingly to cashew nuts. 'Just clothes and style. They had to be in the centre of things – that's a terrible disease.'

'Is it?' asked Mrs Frampton, on whom the cocktails were beginning to work.

'Sure it is. Look, if you need to push into the light all the time it means you ain't a light yourself, ain't that it?'

Mrs Frampton, muddled, agreed.

'How did she do it? Kill him?'

'With a shotgun. Peppered his balls to pieces.'

Both the other women put down their glasses.

'Oh, Lil!' said Caprice di Hudson. 'I never knew *that*!'

'You never knew *why*, eether. There was an awful lot of guessing but it never came out.'

'What? What never came out?'

'That he was in bed with Cilly. Cecilia.'

Caprice di Hudson, for once, was silent. She gazed at Lil Kellogg, her eyes and mouth wide.

'Was that one of the children? The little girl you spoke of?' asked Mrs Frampton. Lil nodded.

'Neet told you?' asked Caprice, her voice unusually quiet.

'Yeah. She took a fall a couple of years ago, knocked the wind out of herself. I guess she thought for a minute there she was on the train to heaven – or the other place. Anyways, I took her into the boathouse, got the full story. I said, Neet, you can't push off leaving me knowing the half of it.'

'Cecilia,' murmured Caprice, shaking her head.

'She said Cilly had been acting quiet for a long time, ever since she and Hal got together. She walked in on it. He'd been sleeping with the kid from the beginning. He slept with both his own girls by his first wife, she said he seemed to think nothing of it, he appeared to believe that women, any woman, any girl, female, was there for him . . . was kind of a . . . was naturally available to him.'

'Gee,' said Caprice di Hudson. There was a short silence.

'The reason she got off with not too much of a sentence was because he coughed about a club for that sort of a thing, messing with children. A lot of well-known men belonged – it was hushed up, they put some of the unimportant ones in jail, just for the look of it. Course, she couldn't inherit his dough, but the kids got it, Tom and Marina that she had by Hal, so they're OK.'

'My word,' said Mrs Frampton. There was a silence and then she said, 'I'd probably have done the same.'

'Me, too,' said Lil Kellogg. 'How about you, Caprice?'

'I was just thinking. I've never been good with guns, though, guess it would have been the nearest heavy instrument except you said he was a big guy – '

'Oh, Hal would never have put up a fight. He was kind of sucked out inside – reared by servants, you know the type. They have to get their own back. Paid for it, though. He lasted three weeks, time for thought, eh?'

'Listen,' said Caprice di Hudson. 'What say we change the subject?'

'OK, but you wanted to know about Neet's past and she sure has one.'

Mrs Frampton, a handful of nuts half-way to her mouth, put them down again, frowning.

How could you say you'd lived without something to look back on? Certainly I wouldn't want a past like that. Just the same, Neet Olafsen had lived. A beauty queen and a model for Worth and Molyneux . . . all those husbands . . . all those children. What sort of past have I got? I have no past.

For a splinter of a second her mind rested on a simple, stone building, shadowed behind a high chalk cliff. And on a man's beautiful back, seen in a mirror on a wall. A vestige of a past, perhaps. Something flickered open again. The brief smell of jasmine and the picture of a woman in a bathing costume . . . a slight woman, with the body of a young girl. Click shut. Mrs Frampton rose abruptly, lifting the jug with the seahorses for a refill.

'Any plans for tomorrow?'

Chapter 25

'DO YOU WANT to pack all these shells?' called Caprice di Hudson.

'Yes!' shouted Mrs Frampton from the bathroom. 'They're for the grandchildren.'

She came into the living-room and looked down at the buckets.

'I hadn't realised there were so many. I'll sort them out.'

She spent half an hour picking out the best and filled a pail with the remainder.

'I'm going down for a last swim.'

'See you on the beach.'

The shore was empty. It was Saturday, the day when people left and new visitors arrived. Mrs Frampton doffed her kimono and strode into the water. As always, it slid against her skin like silk.

You felt caressed. Your feelings melted. You felt cosseted, welcomed by this creamy, delicious sea. No matter how far out you swam, when you returned you were at the same spot. There was no undertow, no tide to take you off course.

This was a benevolent sea – except, she knew, for the rare occasion when the sea reminded, brutally, that it was not a loving servant but a dragon of destruction. She swam out lazily and floated and dived, swam under the surface and floated again. Not a boat in sight. She lay, arms out, face up, eyes closed.

What next? Who knew? There was nothing but the bowl of sea and sky. What next, May?

It was easier to swim. She crawled and backstroked gently, parallel to the shore, and then struck inwards towards a clump of palms. Still no one to be seen. She trod water, and, feeling the gentle slip of shells beneath her, waded ashore. There were no sounds but the gentle whisper of the sea and the murmur of a slight breeze in the casuarinas.

What was that in the water? Grey shapes, now gone, now appearing again. A shoal of dolphins – and so close to the shore! How many? One, two, three, four – and yes, a little one, rising and falling by the side of its mother. They disappeared. Now they were nearer, they had changed direction and were approaching at an angle.

I can see their faces, their eyes! And their mouths, their kindly smiling mouths and gentle snouts!

Mrs Frampton, in her deep-blue costume with the decorous skirt, stood very still. Ah, they were moving away, they wouldn't come any closer, they were already in the shallows. Yes, there they were, further off.

As she watched, one of the dolphins turned, dived and came up again. This time he was close, very close. He seemed to be approaching her. Now the water was so shallow that the animal could not submerge. The regular waves bore him in. He was coming towards her – straight towards her! Mrs Frampton held her breath. There was another small surging roll and the dolphin came surfing in on this, a larger wave. And touched her on the toe. Her mouth dropped open, her eyes wide with wonder as the dolphin receded with the wave, swerved through the shelly surf and dived into deeper water. She watched, breathless, as he rose, and rolled over, and then returned, as if to say farewell before diving and disappearing. She stood for a long while, watching the shapes become vague in the distance. They were gone. There was a movement at her elbow. It was Caprice.

'Did you see?' She could hardly speak.

'I saw it from the top of the bank.'

'He touched me.'

'You're kidding . . . I couldn't see from behind.'

'Oh, Caprice.'

Mrs Frampton, walking up the beach, sat down with a bump and burst into tears. Caprice di Hudson held her in her arms as Mrs Frampton cried for several minutes.

'I'm sorry. I'm being a fool.'

'Come on, don't get smart with yourself. You English are all the same, you can't talk about your feelings. Listen, inhibition is nothing but a cheap shot.'

'I feel a fool,' said Mrs Frampton, digging her wet feet into the sand.

'Because you don't look like Hedy Lamarr and it's only supposed to happen to "thirty-four, twenty-three, thirty-fours"? Come off it, May, where does that put the rest of us . . . the majority?'

Mrs Frampton snivelled, and wiped her nose on her kimono.

'I'm sorry.'

'That's OK. Take your time.'

But she was unable to go on. She was unable to say anything, to make any explanation, to confide in this splendid, successful woman. Who had taken her up, and given her support without demand or question, who had accepted her physical help on the tour but insisted on paying all the expenses, making few demands. They didn't always hit it off. Caprice was, without respite, noisy. Her energy was tiring – she was probably fifteen years younger than Mrs Frampton (her age seemed to vary). She liked to be the centre, she was used to it. But she was never unkind. As well as the lugubrious Ruby, who sent mangled misinformation from New York, there was a raft of other dependants to whom she was a shrewd source of advice, and more.

I've been so lucky, thought Mrs Frampton, rolling up her beach towel. Very lucky.

'Listen,' said Caprice di Hudson, rising. 'There are some fools who won't allow themselves to fall in love because they're afraid of getting hurt. So you get hurt . . . so what?'

She rose, dusting off her skirt, and strode up the beach. Mrs Frampton followed and then paused, seeing a flash of pink.

Ah, one of my shells.

It was a beauty, larger than usual. She gazed at its pink-and-whiteness in the palm of her hand and looked back at the sea.

This one is special.

'What time is the car coming?'

143

'Two o'clock.'

'Good, I've got time to do a picture.'

She spent the rest of the morning on the beach with her box of waterpaints, working furiously, tearing off sheets and discarding, settling again to try for the paleness, the pearly sheen of the day. How the hell could you paint dolphins and not make them look like toilet-paper advertisements? She muttered to herself and when Patti Steinberg came along the beach with her hounds she threw up her hands with a yowl. Patti squatted on her haunches as the dogs dashed off and perused one sheet after another.

'You're painting bigger, that's good.'

Shall I tell her? She found that she had blurted it out anyway.

'A dolphin came right up, right out of the water and touched me on the foot. I was standing just along there at the water's edge. There was a school of them and this one came in and touched me on the foot and rolled over and looked at me and went off again.'

Patti nodded.

'They do that, do they?'

'No. Not normally. They'll come real close to a boat, but no, I'd say that was unusual.'

She looked at the paintings.

'They're just scribbles. I don't know what I'm trying to do, I . . .'

'Well, one thing you could do is quit apologising. Not that they're good.' Patti's pale, bulbous eyes surveyed her. 'You need to work. You don't work enough. What's the point if you don't work at it?'

Mrs Frampton smiled, reassured and deeply flattered. She had spent a day at one of Patti's summer classes. And afterwards, drinking beer, Patti had explained her harshness to some of her pupils.

'I don't bother with the no-goods. I'm kind to them. The good ones – well, they have to get off their asses. You don't get given a talent to leave it in the closet, goddammit.'

'I might as well chuck these,' said Mrs Frampton, gathering up the sheets.

'No, don't do that. Use them to make a good painting out of. Well, to make a lot of bad paintings and a few good accidents.'

'Accidents?'

'The more you work, the more happy accidents you get. Take my word for it. I'll keep this one of the dolphin's head . . . don't worry, it's not the best. Just remember I have it and expect something better next time.'

'Oh, but – '

Something made Mrs Frampton stop. Patti was in her seventies. And looking ahead. So was Neet Olafsen, who had bade her *au revoir* the evening before, whizzing a pack of newspapers past her ear on to the step of the small shop.

Who knows? Perhaps I will come back. Or perhaps I'll go to China. Or Egypt. Or Mars.

Chapter 26

'**D**O YOU MIND?'

'I'm sorry,' said Mrs Frampton. She had been gazing out of the window at the people on Colombia Avenue.

'The salt, I need the salt.'

Mrs Frampton had formed the habit of eating lunch early in order to be sure of the small table under the palm by the window. Today the restaurant was busy and the girls in pink flew about like butterflies. She was cutting into her veal when a little man sat down opposite her, despite an empty table near by. A hunched, wizened creature, his head was now bent over his soup. He looked up and she saw his face, a sharp face, with dark eyes. He salted his soup liberally, and caught her glance.

'Bad for you, huh?'

'Very bad for you.'

'You're English! I was there during the war. First in Lincoln and after on the south coast – Christchurch, do you know it?'

'You were in the war?'

'I was a fighter pilot. Remember the buzz bombs? Been a lot more of them if we hadn't bombed the hell outa the sites. Low-level stuff, we lost a lot of men.'

He bent, unconcerned, to his soup, finished it and sat back as Mrs Frampton stirred at her plate with a fork.

'That's not a lunch, that's for a pigeon. You dieting?'

'I'm not very hungry.'

He looked at her with his button eyes.

'Wassa matter, your husband took off with a younger woman?'

'No such luck,' said Mrs Frampton. And laughed.

'You look nice,' he said.

'I'm a widow,' said Mrs Frampton.

146

His main course, chicken with dumplings and hearty side dishes of root vegetables, arrived. His attention reverted to his lunch and Mrs Frampton returned to her window-gazing.

How beautiful they are, the young! I don't remember us being so nice-looking. Nowadays they all seem to have wonderful skins, long legs, shining hair and teeth. Perhaps it's because when you get old everything becomes so faded and discoloured.

She crumbled a roll on to the cloth, rolling the crumbs into tiny balls, as was her habit. The dentine on your teeth went, so they lost their whiteness – thank God, at least, for her wiry hair, but even that was not so thick as it was.

It's more manageable, May. Still.

And there was something wrong with her feet. The left arch was painful.

If I can't walk, what shall I do?

During the week, since their return from Florida, Caprice busy with affairs, she had been walking the streets of New York, her vitality strengthened both from the sun and the sea and from the strange energy that seemed to seep up between the paving stones of New York City. You had so much go! What was it? Was it the harsh East Coast air, or something to do with the people?

'Penny for your thoughts,' said the man opposite.

'I was wondering,' said Mrs Frampton, demolishing the remains of her roll, 'where all the energy came from. Here. In New York.'

The little man grunted, tackling his lunch as though his attention could not be too much diverted from his plate. She watched him dissect the last pieces of chicken from the bone and asked, 'Are you a surgeon?'

'I coulda bin.'

He chewed purposefully, finished off his baked parsnips, the skin of his jacket potato, and, with half a roll, wiped his plate clean. Not for the first time Mrs Frampton pondered on New York manners.

They behave like starving peasants still. No one says please or thank you, and if you do they look at you in baffled surprise, or suspicion.

147

Even at the receptions after Caprice's public appearances people pushed and shoved towards the food like disaster victims. Once she had been elbowed aside by a Senator and his wife, only to cannon into an elderly movie star who had glared and pushed past, his plate piled high.

Her table companion wiped his mouth forcefully with his napkin and looked across at Mrs Frampton's plate.

'You don't wannit, you don't like it? Change it. Here, over here, miss . . .'

'No!' cried Mrs Frampton, putting out a restraining hand. 'There's nothing wrong with it, please.'

'Not hungry, huh? So wassa matter?'

Mrs Frampton, ruffled, made no answer.

Really. They walked straight in on you – how old were you, how much were you worth, what was your weight – I'll never get used to it.

'I figured you for a troubled person the minute I saw you.'

Oh, did he!

He waved an imperious hand for his bill.

'Miss, can I get the check, I don't have all day. I'll tell you where the energy comes from, lady. It comes from us.'

'I'm sorry?'

'Don't be. It comes from the people. You new to New York?'

'Yes.'

'This town . . . this town is like a medieval city. Like it was in the time of the Medicis – get me?'

Mrs Frampton's eyes opened as she looked at him for the first time with interest. What a funny little man. The Medicis!

'All the time people are pushing up from the bottom – first the Irish, the Italians, the Jews . . . I'm a Jew, I was born in Cracow, my family left when I was four years old.'

'Oh, really?'

'Then the blacks, now the Puerto Ricans, the Cubans, the Chicanos . . . even the Russians . . . everybody reaching for the good time, the top of the heap, the banquet. You here as a tourist?'

'I came to see my son and his family.'

'What's he do?'

'He's a scientist.'

'Medicine, industrial, what?'

'Michael works in medicine. In research. In Boston. At the moment he's in Australia.'

'So you're taking time off in New York? Where are you staying, you staying on the west side?'

'I'm sharing an apartment with a friend.'

'Oh, you're with a friend? Male or female?'

'I'm the guest of Mrs di Hudson, the – '

'Caprice di Hudson? No kidding!'

So much for you, nosy, thought Mrs Frampton.

'And what about you, Mr – I'm sorry, I don't know your name.'

'Sam Wolff. Here – my card.'

She took the card and read 'Samuel E. Wolff' with an east-side address. She made to return it.

'Keep it. Put it in your purse.'

Mrs Frampton, out of *politesse*, did as she was bidden.

'What are you going to do now, a little shopping? I know you ladies like shopping.'

Mrs Frampton regarded him frostily.

'I thought I'd take a walk across Central Park.'

'Great, I'll join you.'

The day was cold, a day to walk briskly. Sam Wolff kept up an acerbic conversation which Mrs Frampton did not find unpleasant. It was useful to have someone who knew the city so well. The little man, barely her own height, pointed out buildings, with an anecdote for each of them.

'And this is the Met – the Metropolitan Museum. D'ya like paintings?'

'I paint myself, as a matter of fact,' said Mrs Frampton loftily, picking up a condescension in his tone.

'You do, huh? Yeah, I bet.' This last was said almost to himself.

Oh, we know what you're thinking. Kittens in a basket, with blue bows, that's what I'm down for.

'What's your style?'

Armed by Patti Steinberg, Mrs Frampton replied coolly, 'Oh, I'm really out of fashion. I'm still with abstract expressionism.'

'You like that stuff, eh?'

'Take a look,' said Mrs Frampton, pointing up at the scudding cirro-cumulus. The little man stopped in his tracks, squinted up and laughed aloud, beating a gloved hand against his thigh.

'What you say your name was?'

'Frampton. Mrs Frampton.'

He caught up with her.

'Missus Frampton – what the hell? What's your name . . . your given name?'

'May. May Frampton.'

'May? Well, it's short. I think I had a wife of that name once.'

They crossed the road past the Met and walked through to a busy shopping street.

'Now,' said Sam Wolff, 'prepare to hang on to your plastic. You know this street? It's Madison Avenue, never knew a woman could resist it.'

Within half an hour he had bought Mrs Frampton a large posy of violets, a round box of chocolates he called candy, and, after a mutual browse, a well-produced book of Manet's paintings.

'I can't take this,' protested Mrs Frampton, noting the price.

'Go on, take it. This is our first date, it's all you're gonna get.'

First date! Despite herself, Mrs Frampton grinned as she was shepherded into a quiet and lavishly appointed tea-room at the back of a *pâtisserie*.

He certainly knows his way around . . . probably brings all his pick-ups here.

'I bet you think I bring all my pick-ups here, huh?'

Mrs Frampton, slightly shaken, sat down abruptly. She covered by saying, 'You know, I don't think I could have walked another step.'

'You won't have to.'

'I couldn't if I tried – you'd have to wheel me off in that trolley.'

He called the waitress with his impossible rudeness, and, without consulting her, ordered tea and cakes.

'You'll like 'em, don't fuss me, I know this place. You don't like 'em, we'll go to the Pierre, the Carlyle, wherever you want.'

Mrs Frampton shook her head. You couldn't keep up with him. He had a nice nose, long. Like a ski slope. She slid another look as he sat back in his chair, preening.

Catching her at it, he grinned triumphantly and leaned forward, perusing her face.

'You got a great skin, May. Anybody ever tell you that?'

'No.'

'Fine eyes, too.'

The girl came with the tray. Mrs Frampton, thoroughly disturbed, leaned towards the pot. He beat her to it.

'How d'ya wannit?'

'Milk, no sugar.'

He poured, and handed her the cup, and then the plate of cakes. She shook her head and he handed her an arrangement of sandwiches, cut into small triangles. She sat with her head down.

'OK. So tell me.'

She looked up at him, her eyes dark

Chapter 27

'LOOK, I MUST ring Caprice,' said Mrs Frampton. 'She'll wonder where I am.'

'OK,' said Sam Wolff. 'Then I'll take you for a night tour of Manhattan.'

'No more walking?'

'No more walking.'

He shouted, 'Waiter, can you gimmee a phone?'

The waiter brought a telephone to the table at once. Mrs Frampton, usually intimidated by grand hotels, had discovered earlier that this was not necessary in America. Most Americans, it seemed, did not want to intimidate. She had discussed this with Caprice who had agreed it was true. People were dropped, snubbed, sure, in grand circles. But the English way of condescension, of deadeningly exclusive over-politeness, was almost non-existent. You might know your stock was down at any given moment. But it could be up a year later. She rang Caprice.

'There's no reply, she must still be with her business manager.'

'Let's go.'

He did at least stand behind her chair to help her up. Wasn't he going to pay the bill? A waiter came forward and the little man signed.

'Good-night, Mr Wolff, good-night, madam.'

'They seem to know you here.'

'Sure they do.'

Outside on the pavement he jiggled about, shrugging into his coat, ignoring her attempts to assist. An enormous black limousine drew up.

'Come on.'

The chauffeur got out and held the door.

152

'Come on, get in.'

In the car she asked, 'Mr Wolff, is this your car?'

'Sure. I told you, call me Sam.'

Mrs Frampton sat back against the leather upholstery.

'What make is it?'

'So it's a limey car, so what? I have a weakness. Take us down Broadway, Mark.'

The car purred round by the Plaza Hotel, along the south side of the park, and took a left.

'You know Broadway?'

'Caprice and I walked down one afternoon. Not at night, though.'

'Looks better at night, you don't see the sleaze.'

They slowed in Times Square, then drove over to the Hudson and the Village, and back up Fifth Avenue.

'I've never seen so many rich-looking people!' cried Mrs Frampton, her nose to the window.

'Nor so many hobos. Listen, I know a good place for a nightcap.'

They stopped in a side street. In the bar a pianist played the blues. Sam Wolff ordered brandies.

'I don't know if I want this.'

'Medicinal.'

Mrs Frampton looked at him and saw that his eyes were kind.

'Yes,' she said, and, at his impatient nod, obediently drank the brandy.

When Caprice arrived home at midnight, full of wine and apologies, Mrs Frampton was sitting in the drawing-room with a bemused expression on her face.

'I rang in but you were out. Did you get my message on the machine?'

'Yes, I was out, too. I met someone.'

'Oh? A friend?'

'No. I got picked up.'

'Hey, be careful!'

'You won't believe it,' said Mrs Frampton. 'I met this little man in Alfredo's, he came and sat at my table . . . I still can't believe it all happened.'

'What . . . what happened?'

'Ohh . . .'

It was impossible to say to Caprice that she had sat in a tea-room for two hours pouring out the pain of the last three years of her life to a complete stranger. She had never confided in Caprice, not even when Caprice had openly invited it, suggesting that sharing was good for the soul. It had been an impossibility, the time was not right.

'We walked across the park together. We saw some of Madison Avenue, had tea . . . had dinner at the Carlyle – '

'Hey – yow!' said Caprice di Hudson.

' – then he took me for a ride in his limousine . . . with a chauffeur, he has a chauffeur. Then we had a brandy in a bar. Then he brought me home.'

'What's his name?'

'Sam. Sam Wolff.'

'Not *the* Sam Wolff?'

'I don't know. Who is he?'

'Sam Wolff? Industrialist . . . he was a chemist, inventor, something. Now he has fingers in everything, he's a friend of the President.'

'I don't think it can be the same man,' said Mrs Frampton.

'You know what I feel like?' said Caprice di Hudson. 'Hot chocolate.'

In the kitchen Caprice returned to the little man.

'What does he look like?'

'Very short, long head like a spoon, *very* bright eyes, loud voice, no hair on top, grey round the sides, big black eyebrows.'

'That sounds like Sam Wolff,' said Caprice, pausing at the stove. 'Are you seeing him again?'

'I don't know,' said Mrs Frampton. 'I'm not sure how we left it.' She pondered for a moment. 'They certainly knew him at the hotel. They were all over him.'

'What I don't understand,' said Caprice, 'is what he was doing in Alfredo's. Not his sort of joint.'

'Well, I've no idea. I was looking out of the window and he went by.'

'Did he look in as he passed? I mean, did your eyes meet, that kind of thing?'

'As a matter of fact, they did. I remember thinking: *He* looks Jewish, and I liked his coat. The next thing I knew he was sitting down opposite me.'

At nine o'clock the next morning Caprice's doorbell rang. The maid came into the breakfast room with an enormous bouquet of deep, crimson roses.

'There's five dozen here, Miz Frampton – that's a big bunch of roses you got there.'

Caprice, emerging from her bathroom, came forward for a closer look.

'My God, May – you've made a conquest.'

'Come on!'

'I certainly don't think it's simply olde-worlde courtesy . . . not from what you said about him. I reckon he's after your body.' She grinned her delicious grin and disappeared back to the bathroom, carolling a love song.

Almost immediately the telephone rang. Sam Wolff was on the line.

'D'ya get my flowers?'

'They've just arrived, yes. Thank you. Thank you very much. The maid is just putting them in water.'

'D'you wanna see the delicatessen I was telling you about . . . the one down the road?'

Mrs Frampton, flustered, said yes to get him off the line.

Her liver was hardly awake yet, so that she was in no mood for decision-making. As she put down the telephone Caprice re-emerged, her hair dripping from the shower.

'Was it him?'

'Yes! He wants me to go out with him again.' She stood, in the middle of the enormous sitting-room, gazing round vaguely at the pictures on the wall. 'I mean . . . is this usual?'

Caprice di Hudson gave her an old-fashioned look.

'I'll get on the phone, find out more about the guy, if it'll

155

make you feel more comfortable. What did you have in mind to wear?'

'Ooh, Lord!' groaned Mrs Frampton.

'I'll take the malossol and the beluga . . . nah, nah, nah, the big tins . . .'

'OK, Mr Wolff, whatever you say, Mr Wolff, sir.'

'And some of the salmon eggs, the pink – I guess maybe that's the one she'll prefer, I know what women like.'

'You sure do, Mr Wolff, you sure do.'

Mrs Frampton, in her green suede coat with the big buttons, crushed and pressed by the crowds in the vast, bewildering delicatessen, listened to this conversation with increasing irritation. Who on earth did this little twerp think he was? And what . . . *what* had the assistant just said? Could she have heard aright?

'That will be six hundred dollars, Mr Wolff, sir.'

Six hundred dollars? Was it a joke between them? Six hundred dollars?!

Battered by a Manhattan matron who rammed her against a tub of giant salamis and then shouted above her head at a younger facsimile, obviously her daughter, as though Mrs Frampton did not exist, she used her elbows forcefully and struggled after the little man who had disappeared entirely in the crush. With difficulty she made her way to the door and after a while he appeared at her elbow.

'Some place, huh, Zabar's? The best in town. Fast turnover so fresh stock, you get the best. You wanna walk?'

'I don't mind,' said Mrs Frampton, recovering her humour in the crisp white air. There was a mild sunshine that caught the edges of roofs and the frosting of snow turned them into Monets. She breathed deep.

'Be careful!'

The little man drew her back violently as a young man lurched towards her.

'Drugs,' said Sam Wolff flatly, and they crossed the street, leaving Mark in the Rolls to follow.

'What did you mean?'

'The guy was an addict. He was after your purse. You have to watch out for yourself. You shouldn't walk the streets alone. Not now. Three years ago, two, maybe, yes, in daylight. Not now. Now, ring for a cab, even if it's only three blocks.'

Mrs Frampton was silent, digesting this frightfulness. After they had walked a while, the Rolls moved up silently beside them and he ushered her in impatiently. They drove slowly through the park, and she was glad of the warmth of the car. On the east side they turned north for two blocks and drew up before a large brownstone house with a glass porch and beautiful bronzework. Sam Wolff, neglecting to help her out, rushed into the building, leaving her to Mark, the chauffeur. In the lobby a tall old man in a striped waistcoat was taking Sam Wolff's coat. He turned to help Mrs Frampton, taking her suede from her. Sam Wolff snatched it from him.

'This coat is not warm enough. You're gonna get a cold on your kidneys.'

'I *was* feeling cold,' said Mrs Frampton, following him up a broad stairway and across wide polished wood into a large room. Everything was wood. The walls were clad, and here and there were paintings, mostly of the Dutch school, mellow and resonant, their colours at home in the muted room.

'Let's eat.'

After a moment the butler brought silver trays with bread and butter, and chopped egg and onion.

'I don't care for all this stuff, but maybe you will,' said Sam Wolff grudgingly. 'Here.'

He handed her a broad, short fork and without waiting opened up a tin of caviar and began to shovel it in. Mrs Frampton, after a second, began to taste, first one and then another.

'You like the pink best, huh?'

'No,' said Mrs Frampton. 'I like them all. This one the most.'

She tapped the tin with the soft grey eggs.

'The beluga, eh? You're gonna cost me.'

'If I were eating, I don't know, informally, with other things or as a garnish, I'd use the salmon eggs, they're prettier. And yes, they are nice . . . it's like eating little eggs of . . . not sea water, exactly, but some distillation of the sea.'

'The woman's a poet,' said Sam Wolff drily to the hovering butler, who smiled and withdrew.

'Is this your house?'

'What do you think of it?'

'Very nice. Quiet. Austere.'

'You expected Barnum and Bailey – go on, admit it!'

'You didn't tell me you were going to bring me to your house.'

'Home . . . home! In America a house is something else.'

'Oh,' said Mrs Frampton, going pink with an idea of what he meant. 'The pictures look well here.'

'They're not the best, those are in the vaults or in museums.'

'May Liu, my friend, had wonderful pictures.'

How marvellous, to be able to say that! To speak that name, utter the name of her beloved to this crochety creature, this . . . this elf. To whom she had told everything.

To her surprise he said, 'I know. I sold her the Matisse, the one with the blue and pink and yellow, I tried to get it back but she wouldn't have it. I never should have sold it.'

'She left it to me in her will.'

'Good, I'll buy it from you.'

'It's going to auction. They're waiting for the right time.'

'Name your price.'

'I can't, Sam.' It was the first time she had used his name and his heavy eyebrows rose like starlings and he smiled briefly.

'Why not?'

'I must get a good price, I've promised the money to the foundation.'

'We'll talk about it.'

The butler came back with a tray of tea.

'Whaddya know?' said Sam Wolff. 'Nice big English Worcester cups. This man knows how to treat a veddy, veddy British broad, eh?'

He snickered away, pouring the tea and handing it to her with mock gallantry. Then he came and sat beside her on the sofa.

And gazed as she sipped. As she put her cup down he patted her hand.

'You're a very attractive woman, May.'

And what is the point of that, she thought, if I'm only attractive to the likes of you? Is he having me on? She slid a look at him. He didn't look so bad this morning, particularly in the soft light, and sitting down. It was a nice face in a way. A bit devilish.

I bet you're a rogue, she thought . . . oh, you're a rogue all right, you're like the gypsies and poachers back home.

'You're right,' he said suddenly, making her jump. 'I'm no angel.'

Was he clairvoyant as well?

'That must be useful to you – in business. Reading other people's thoughts.'

His answer to that was to knock her backwards on the sofa and kiss her deeply and greedily with fishy lips. She was too surprised to do anything, but then she struggled up from the engulfing cushions, red-faced and upset.

'Mr Wolff!'

She rose, trying to straighten her skirt.

'Look, I think we'd better sort this out. I don't know who you think I am –'

'I know who you are, you told me. You're a nurse, your husband took off with some kvetch of a Frenchwoman who – '

'That's enough! I've had enough! Where's my coat?'

'Wassa matter, wassa matter with you . . .? I'm just getting started, we're just getting the relationship started here – '

'Relationship? What relationship?'

'Our relationship, you stupid . . . OK, OK, listen, how long do you think we both got? I could fall down in the street tomorrow. Come and sit down . . . OK, OK, you're English, I got to hold back, you're frigid English – sit down, for Christ's sake, you're making my neck ache.'

Mrs Frampton, concerned by the whereabouts of her coat, sat heavily in a large brown armchair, at a distance from the sofa.

'Listen,' he said, rising and walking back and forth with an amazingly light step. 'Listen, I can have any woman I want. I can buy a twenty-five year old, make babies if I want.'

'Why don't you, then?'

'I got children,' he said so darkly that Mrs Frampton burst out giggling. He looked at her, then nodded slowly.

'You got it.'

He stood, jingling something in his pocket.

'I can't think what you want with me,' said Mrs Frampton, playing with the fringe on the arm of the chair.

'Oh, now she wants the compliments. OK, so you got a nice skin, I like your voice, I like the way you speak low.'

'I learned that in nursing,' said Mrs Frampton.

'Yeah, well, like I say, nice.'

There was a little silence. The room was very shadowy, with heavy net curtains diffusing the light. Sam Wolff stood there jingling. Then he turned towards her slightly.

'I looked in the window. You were looking out. It was your face. I thought: Sam, there's work here.'

'What do you mean, work?'

'You made a signal to me. An unhappiness signal.'

'No, I didn't. I was just looking out of the window.'

'My sister looked the same when her kid was killed in a car smash.'

'I see. You mean you felt sorry for me?'

'No, dummy. I mean I want to go to bed with you. I want to cuddle up.'

'Oh rats,' said Mrs Frampton.

'I know what we need,' he said. 'Champagne. Pink champagne.'

Chapter 28

LUISA, CAPRICE'S MAID, shook Mrs Frampton awake.
'Telephone.'
'Is it . . .?'
'Yuh, it's him.'
Mrs Frampton yawned and stretched and sat up. She shook
her head and breathed deep to wake herself, and picked up the
telephone.
'Are you ready?'
'No, I'm still asleep, I'm in bed.'
'I gotta surprise for you.'
'Not another fur coat?'
There had been a tussle over the coat. He had appeared one
morning with a beautiful coat over his arm. She had smoothed
it lovingly. And told him that she disapproved of fur coats. He
had yelled that she was prepared to wear leather and eat meat.
And taken the coat away.
'No, it's not another fur coat and quit the nagging. I'll pick
you up at midday. This is a special occasion so don't come
looking like the cleaning lady.'
'Thanks,' she said, and hung up.
Why on earth did I tell him everything? she wondered crossly.
Now he thinks he knows all about me. He thinks I'm in his
pocket – for as long as it amuses him. Well, there's the matter
of my amusement, too. I'm a free agent.
She took a leisurely bath in Caprice's huge bathroom, washing
and pinning up her hair.
I'll wear it up at the back with combs. It was getting long,
but at least it gave you a choice.
What to wear was as difficult as ever. She had meant to shop, and
sizing was easy, since wherever you went, they had your size.

Here, if you have the dough . . . Good grief, I'm beginning to think like them . . . If you have the money, you have the choice.

In the end she put on a brown wool dress bought to keep out the cold winds of Chicago, and pinned on an orange glass brooch she had found in Fort Myers in Florida.

'Caprice! May I borrow the hat?'

The hat was a darling, a mixture of nylon and mohair that looked like fur and hugged the head, swirling so that your hair and the hat were one. It made her eyes look a good colour. In the lobby, waiting for the limousine, she caught sight of herself in the slip mirror by the elevator.

Hello, I look up to mischief.

It was true. She looked young. Any age. The lines between her nose and mouth seemed to have disappeared. Mark looked in and held open the wide doors for her.

'Mr Wolff had an appointment. He'll be there to meet you.'

'Where are we going?'

'Didn't he say? To the Met.'

When they got to the Metropolitan there were cameramen on the steps of the museum. She walked into the lobby and Sam at once detached himself from a large group of people.

'Private show,' he hissed in her ear, 'for the over-rich and the over-privileged. Do you wanna meet – ?'

Mrs Frampton, with one glance at the formidable, elegant groups, shook her head.

'No thanks.'

'You're right, they're boring as hell. Come on.'

'Is it the Van Gogh?' She had seen the posters all over New York.

'Yeah. Now listen, I have to go someplace. I'll give you two hours and meet you at the exit to the show, in the shop.'

Two hours?

She turned to remonstrate but he was gone. Someone gave her a heavy and ornamented catalogue. Crowds surged in the foyer, and waiters squeezed and shouldered their way with

162

drinks and canapés. Alone, and too nervous to join in, Mrs Frampton turned and entered the almost empty galleries.

Inside she glanced at the preamble in the catalogue. These were the pictures painted by Van Gogh in the last eighteen months of his life. That seemed a silly gimmick. They probably weren't going to be the best. The man was ill, wasn't he? Confined? By this time she had strolled into the gallery proper.

Time disappeared. Her body disappeared. It was as if she became only eyes, a seeing mechanism, as if her whole body was transformed into a looking machine. As she moved from one painting to the next, it was as if she were the painter, making the decisions, laying on the strokes, feeling the brush under her hand. It seemed as though paint, painting, had just been discovered, as if all the modes, all learning, had come together in one bright, bold, unified intellectual thought-feeling. The trees were so powerful that she had to close her eyes. They made her physically faint. They showed too much, more than human beings were programmed to receive. There were small secondary images, strange faces peering from the branches, reminders of something, somewhere, just beyond consciousness. The incense cypress whorled and writhed in a pain of movement. The chrome-yellow roofs, the pink madder streets, were familiar and yet at the same time as never seen before, an enlargement, a gift of enrichment. And everything without fault. There were no mistakes!

I know what it was, he knew he had no time. There was no time for error, for sidepaths, for experiment. He had to get it down. He had to get it right.

She stood for a long time in front of a painting of a boat on water, with people, and trees beyond. And even longer before a painting of trees in verdant spring, with a man and a woman walking.

It is everything I know, she thought . . . everything I have ever learned, all brought together in one canvas. Things grow. And won't be forsworn. It is ecstasy. Everything, all of it, worth it for this ecstasy.

The tears rolled down her face and people stared at her. She moved on, unawares, and when she had reached the last painting she went back to the beginning and read the paintings again, slowly and carefully.

Why are the colours so fresh, as fresh, surely, as the day they were painted?

She looked at two pictures of a street, hung side by side, one slightly more gentle, the other brutal in its apperception.

Bet they've reproduced the gentle one.

In the end, her back suddenly on fire, she walked slowly and stiffly from the museum to the large shop where the reproductions were on sale. Sam Wolff stepped forward and took her by the elbow. She shook her head slightly, unable to speak.

'Don't worry, I ordered all the reproductions, you can look at them as long as you want. Put 'em in plain frames, not fancy like in there – he wanted plain, it's recorded.'

In the car she turned to him and said, 'Sam, I think I have to go back to Europe.'

'Sure you do.'

'I need . . .' What did she need?

'You going to sell the farm?'

'Yes. Yes, I'm going to sell it. With all the improvements I think I might do well out of it. People are looking for places behind the coast.'

'Where yah gonna live?'

'Lord knows. Somewhere warmish. Not too isolated. Somewhere I can see the sea.'

He sat, scratching his hands, one of his many mannerisms.

'Any ideas?'

'You asking me? Sure I got ideas. I'm full of ideas. Hey, Mark . . .'

He leaned forward and gave the chauffeur instructions on a restaurant for lunch.

'You feel like Italian?'

'Why not?'

He leaned back, sucking his top lip.

'How about Menton?'

'Menton?'

'It's warm. Peaceful. Kind of faded . . .' he conceded.

'That should suit me, then,' she said drily, making him mutter

. . . She knew he hated the English habit of self-deprecation. She laughed.

'Near Italy,' he said. 'For the grand tour you keep talking about. You got a lot of looking to do.'

'I know. It's probably a good idea. Somewhere quiet, un-aggressive.'

'You'll like it, it's a nice place, nice pool, house in the Italian style, good gardens, they need a little attention – '

'I don't understand. You mean you have a house there?'

'Sure I have a place there – what do you take me for, some kind of a renter?'

'You didn't say.'

'It's a good house.'

'Then I'd be glad to lease it, while I'm looking around.'

Again he muttered.

'If the rent is not too exorbitant.'

'Long words, long words, get your head out of the dictionary.'

The car purred down Park Avenue, turned and pulled up outside a discreetly painted front. Inside they were received with joyful attention.

'Listen,' said Sam Wolff. 'You know what I requested, so – '

'This way, Mr Wolff.'

They were led through the main restaurant to a mezzanine, where there were secluded booths.

'I booked them all,' said Sam Wolff grandly, taking off his coat and scarf. She never knew whether to believe him when he said things like this.

'Here, siddown.'

He took her coat and she slid into her seat. The paintings still invaded and she could find nothing to say. So she sat across from him, smiling, her face still dazed. Once she put out a hand and gripped his for a moment. And looked away and down at the people below. The waiter took their orders without the usual fuss – had he arranged that, too? – running quickly downstairs.

Sam Wolff leaned forward, and pulled at the shining orange flower on her dress.

'Glass,' she said. 'From a Florida gift shop.'

He nodded and rose abruptly and left, hopping away in his light-footed manner. She watched his wordless exit in surprise. The waiter returned. Mrs Frampton threw up her hands amiably and ordered a glass of Evian water without ice. She waited for half an hour, watching the people below and thinking about the pictures, remembering details, recording colours in her mind. No one else came up to the mezzanine – could he really have meant that he had booked all the tables? But that was silly. Suddenly he was on the stairs again, his bald head gleaming as he came up the steps in a rush. He sat down opposite her, out of breath.

'Sorry it took so long.'

Out of his pocket he fished two brown shiny boxes with gold writing and moved them across the table towards her. She looked at him in surprise. He pushed the larger box forward, so she picked it up. Inside was a lake of fire. She lifted the necklace of golden cabochon stones, which flashed with light. Her mouth opened.

'What are they?' She held the rivière up in her hand, turning it so that the stones flashed.

'Fire opals. Foiled in gold – shows off the colour.'

'Sam, they're . . .!'

But there were no words to express the living, golden snake in her hands. She put the necklace down on the table and they both leaned forward, gazing at the golden depths under the roof lights. He rose and slid out of his seat and she inclined her neck for him to put on the necklace. She touched it gently, then got up and walked to the head of the stairs where there was a looking-glass. The stones made her eyes look yellow. They made her hair dark, and her skin alive.

I don't look a day over forty in this light! It's not that you seek to be what you aren't. Just the same!

She looked back and he was sitting at the table, his head craned towards her. She walked back and sat across from him.

'What can I say?'

'You could say thank you, you ignorant Brit,' he growled.

'Oh, Sam!' She grasped both his hands. 'Yes. Thank you.

166

But that's so inadequate . . . Where did you find them, how did you know they'd be so . . . They're . . . they're just . . . I mean, did you go out . . .?' She shrugged helplessly as words failed her, and touched the stones at her neck, wanting to see them again.

He smiled his smug little smile.

'Nah, nah, nah. I had something else in mind.'

Now he pushed the smaller box which she had forgotten towards her. And watched her as she opened it. Just before she did, she looked up and caught something in his gaze, making him drop his eyes. Inside the box was a ring. Of two stones, large and oblong. A sapphire and an emerald, side by side. She looked down, mesmerised, her head suddenly singing with shock. Blue and green, together. She had never seen that in a ring before. And yet, when she was young, she had wanted, yearned for, a blue-and-green ring after reading of Arthur and Guinevere. The blue of the sea and the green of the land, the colours which meant the most to her, the colours she used in her paintings. How could he know that? He couldn't. She looked up at him. And he looked back, out of his dark eyes.

'Well?'

But she could not answer him. She looked down at the ring, feeling frightened. He leaned forward, took the ring and put it slowly on the third finger of her left hand.

'OK?'

She did not reply.

'So we're engaged? That go with you?'

Mrs Frampton gazed at him.

I'm gawping – close your mouth, you silly woman, you must look like an idiot.

'The opals were an afterthought . . . I paid too much for them, the guy took advantage but what the hell, who cares, you can't go about wearing glass, not with me you can't, anyway, you're too old for fake jewellery.'

She made to say, Thanks, sarcastically, but nothing came out, her throat seemed to be seized up. She touched the ring with her right forefinger and he answered her unspoken query in his frightening way.

167

'The ring I had made up for you. The size was a problem but I figured it right, huh?'

She swivelled the ring. It was proud, but not too tight.

'Sticks a little? Don't worry, lose a little weight.' And, as she pulled a face, 'You're fine by me but the doctors here, they'll want fifteen pounds off you, for sure.'

Mrs Frampton was now totally dazed. Her head was filled with paint, with fiery, glowing stones, and with blue and green.

She looked at him with a careful look and said in a funny voice, 'I think you must be Merlin.'

This made him cackle, and shout for the waiter.

I know what he's doing, she thought. He's reassuring me, playing the fool. He plays the fool. He's so bright he even frightens himself. He doesn't know how to live with it. He drives people potty. It's always been like this. Oh, you poor bugger.

She leaned over the table and put a hand on his shoulder.

'Just one thing. Why me, Sam?'

'Why you? Because you're a mensch.'

'What's that?'

'Who knows? You must be for real, it certainly ain't for your figure, that's for sure.'

'Thanks. Thanks very much.'

She made a mock-punching fist at him and he snickered, and yelled again for the waiters. As they came running, Mrs Frampton sat back in her seat, sighing at the loudness of his voice and turning the ring on her finger.

'Champagne?'

She nodded, though it gave her gas, and the waiters, picking up the excitement, dashed away.

Mrs Frampton leaned forward over the table and stretched out her left hand, displaying the ring. He inspected it gravely, nodding his head with satisfaction. There was a silence of mutual satisfaction. Mrs Frampton sat back.

'Tell me about Menton.'